W9-BUQ-839

THE
SOUND OF LIFE
AND EVERYTHING

THE
SOUND OF LIFE
AND EVERYTHING

Krista Van Dolzer

G. P. Putnam's Sons
An Imprint of Penguin Group (USA)

G. P. Putnam's Sons
Published by the Penguin Group
Penguin Group (USA) LLC
375 Hudson Street
New York, NY 10014

USA | Canada | UK | Ireland | Australia
New Zealand | India | South Africa | China
penguin.com
A Penguin Random House Company

Library of Congress Cataloging-in-Publication Data
Van Dolzer, Krista.
The sound of life and everything / Krista Van Dolzer.
pages cm
Summary: In 1950s California, grieving Mildred Clausen tries to have her son,
who was killed in World War II, cloned, but instead, a Japanese man emerges
and her niece, Ella Mae, befriends him, in spite of the town's intense prejudice
and her aunt's conviction that he is her son's killer.
[1. Family life—California—Fiction. 2. Prejudices—Fiction.
3. Japanese—California—Fiction. 4. Cloning—Fiction.
5. California—History—20th century—Fiction.] I. Title.
PZ7.V2737Sou 2015   [Fic]—dc23   2014015975

Printed in the United States of America.
ISBN 978-0-399-16775-1
1 3 5 7 9 10 8 6 4 2

Design by Annie Ericsson.
Text set in Figural Std.

For Chris and Mom,
who keep me sane

1

Mama said it was plum foolish not to wash the blood off Robby's dog tags. "It's like your auntie thinks that blood will keep your cousin with her, and we both know that's plum foolish." She shook a finger in my face. "And don't you let anyone tell you any differently. Especially Auntie Mildred."

But that was exactly what Auntie Mildred told me. "It's not plum foolishness, it's science." She gave her broom a flick. "I saw this piece just yesterday about a scientist up north. Did you know he can regrow folks from practically nothing?"

But when I got back to the house and reported this news to Mama, she didn't take it seriously. "It was hardly a piece. Auntie Mildred cut that clipping out of yesterday's want ads. If you have a dead man's lock of hair—or a few drops of his blood—some fool doctor wants it for his research." She made a show of sighing. "That ain't science, it's bunk, and if your auntie can't see that, I'm afraid she's gonna end up with a fistful of regrets and a bellyful of heartache."

I could have kept this up, scurrying back and forth

between them like a telegram service, but those two already had enough to fight about, seeing as they were sisters. In fact, when Mama answered the telephone on that sunny Saturday, I figured it was Auntie Mildred calling to resume their never-ending argument about the best way to clean soap scum.

But I was only half right.

"Settle down, Mildred," Mama said. "I can barely understand you."

Auntie Mildred had a habit of shouting into telephones, so I could usually eavesdrop without expending too much effort, but for once, she didn't shout. Her words came out so fast that I could barely catch the gist, and what I caught didn't make sense. Something about Robby and a doctor's appointment, but I couldn't have said how those two things were related. By the time Mama said "All right, we're on our way," I still had no idea what the fuss was about.

"On our way where?" I asked.

Mama hung up the receiver. "That's none of your concern," she replied as she grabbed her gloves.

I folded my arms across my chest. "Then why do I have to come?"

"Because the last time I left you home, you pulled three shelves out of the wall—"

"Well, maybe if you hadn't hidden the snickerdoodles," I said, "I would've been able to reach 'em."

"—and because," Mama went on as if I hadn't cut in, "I

don't want to drive with your auntie by myself. Pasadena's an hour from here."

I scrunched up my nose. "What's in Pasadena?"

"The California Institute of Technology."

"The California *what*?"

"Exactly," Mama said as she steered me out the door.

We walked swiftly to the Clausens' house to pick up Auntie Mildred, Mama's sensible black pumps pounding out a sturdy rhythm on the sunbaked road. Auntie Mildred didn't drive (despite Grandpa Willy's best efforts), but we had to take her car, since the boys had taken ours to go fishing at the pier. I'd wanted to go, too, but Daddy hadn't let me. Apparently, I was too old for manly things like fishing. This morning, I'd been madder than an unmilked dairy cow, but now I thanked my lucky stars. This trip to Pasadena sounded loads more interesting.

"Where's Gracie?" I asked as we climbed into the Clausens' Chrysler. It was actually Uncle George's Chrysler (since he was the only one who drove it), but Auntie Mildred was the one who'd insisted on this model. It was round and teal, a car-shaped dollop of toothpaste.

"Not coming," she said as she pulled on her gloves. Those gloves were so white that they could have been featured on a Rinso commercial whereas Mama's gloves were off-white at best. Mama said that was because Auntie Mildred didn't know how to get her hands dirty.

Mama's golden hair danced in the wind as we thundered

up the street. None of the other ladies at our church knew how to drive, but then, Mama wasn't like any of the other ladies. She'd been raised by Grandpa Willy, who believed in teaching girls how to operate heavy machinery in case they ended up marrying men with no arms and no legs.

It was like Grandpa Willy knew that World War II was coming. He just hadn't realized it would come for his grandsons instead.

The hardworking sun hung an hour lower in the sky when we arrived in Pasadena. Auntie Mildred's knee bounced up and down as she gave Mama directions, but when we finally pulled into the parking lot labeled INGOLSTADT LABORATORIES, she only sat there staring.

Mama threw the gearshift into park. "Well, there's no sense dillydallyin'."

Auntie Mildred looked as wilted as Mr. Whitman's week-old lettuce as she climbed out of the car. I wasn't sure why—it was still cool enough that my legs hadn't stuck to the custom upholstery—but maybe her wilting had less to do with the heat. She gaped at the building, and it gaped back at her. The door was a tightly sealed mouth, and the windows were eyes.

"Pull yourself together," Mama hissed as she dragged her sister to her feet. "If what's inside that building is really what you think it is, will he want to see his mama for the first time in seven years lookin' like the Ghost of Christmas Past?"

"You're right, Anna," she said, tossing her hair over her shoulder. "I need to be strong. For Robby."

"Why for Robby?" I asked. Auntie Mildred didn't make sense on most days, but today, she made even less. Robby was dead and buried, and God and everyone knew it.

But she didn't see fit to grace me with an answer, just let Mama lead her into the lab. They looked like Siamese twins as they half stumbled, half jogged across the crowded parking lot and through the front door. I actually had to sprint to catch up at one point. Wherever we were going, they wanted to get there on the double.

The lobby reminded me of the Alaska Territory (which Miss Fightmaster had covered in her last geography lesson). First, it was enormous. Second, it was cold. And third, except for a reception desk and a three-story portrait mounted on a distant wall, it was completely empty. I didn't recognize the man staring down from the portrait, but he had to be important, since his mug was taking up as much space as our living room.

Mama's booming footsteps made the secretary look up from the paper clips she'd been sorting. "Welcome!" she said brightly as she adjusted her glasses. "Do you have an appointment?"

Auntie Mildred tried to reply, but she just hemmed and hawed. Guess she'd already used up all her words in the car on the way here.

"Yes, ma'am," Mama said, giving me Auntie Mildred's purse. "Ella Mae, would you please find their card?"

Grudgingly, I took the purse. I thought I'd come on this adventure to keep Mama company, not to dig through Auntie Mildred's handkerchiefs and Betty Crocker coupons. I was about to say so, too, when the secretary intervened.

"Oh, don't bother," she said. "We never give out our cards. If you dropped it on the sidewalk, anyone might pick it up, and then where would we be?" She pulled out her appointment book. "I'll just look you up."

Auntie Mildred's mouth moved, but no sound came out.

I pretended not to notice. No need to draw even more attention to my embarrassing kin. "Her name is Mildred Clausen."

The secretary flipped through her appointment book. "Ah, yes, Mildred Clausen, two fifteen with Dr. Franks." She eyed us over her glasses. "Now I just need to see ID."

Auntie Mildred took her purse back, pulled a water bill out of the pocket, and handed it across the desk.

"Thank you, Mrs. Clausen." She set her sights on Mama. "And what about you?"

Mama made no effort to reach for her purse, though I wasn't sure why. It seemed like a reasonable request—Sergeant Friday always asked to see ID on *Dragnet*—but then, Mama was less familiar with due process than I was. She always made a point of darning socks or doing dishes while me and Daddy watched the show together.

The secretary clasped her hands over her appointment book. "I apologize for the inconvenience, but the work we do here at Ingolstadt is of a very sensitive nature." It sounded like something she'd said at least a hundred times.

Mama held out for another moment, then reluctantly dug out her wallet and slapped her driver's license on the desk.

The secretary made a show of reading every word. "Thank you, Mrs. Higbee."

Mama stuffed it into her wallet. "What about my daughter? Are you afraid my Ella Mae's not who she says she is?"

The secretary forced a smile. "Of course not, Mrs. Higbee." She motioned toward a silver door at the far end of the lobby. "You can go in now."

Mama didn't smile back as she hurried us away, black pumps thumping impatiently across the shiny tiles. A large man in a black suit was waiting by the door, and I felt my pulse quicken. If the man thought he could stop us, he was in for a surprise. Once Mama made her mind up, she didn't often change it. But he didn't try to slow us down. When the silver door slid open, he waved us right through.

On the other side of the door, we found another lobby, slightly smaller, and another secretary, this one blond-haired (though her hair didn't look quite as natural as Mama's). I assumed she'd dyed it with one of those boxes of Clairol.

"Mrs. Clausen?" she asked.

Auntie Mildred nodded.

"I'm afraid I have to ask to see your ID again."

Mama threw her arms up. "Who do you think you are, the FBI?"

The secretary smiled ruefully. "And yours, too, Mrs. Higbee."

After this secretary determined that Mama and Auntie Mildred hadn't somehow switched identities in the last twenty-three seconds, she motioned toward another door at the far end of this lobby. It was guarded by a slightly larger man in a slightly blacker suit.

We repeated this process another six times, until we were so lost we'd probably need a compass to find our way back out. The lobbies kept getting smaller, as if the walls themselves were closing in around us, and the secretaries kept getting softer, as if they were afraid to breathe. The last one didn't say anything, just glanced at our IDs and led us into a labyrinth of narrow, twisty halls. She left us in a small white room with a large screen and a red door.

I'd been anxious to see what the men were guarding, and now that we were here, it was hard to make myself sit still. At least we only had to wait a few minutes before the door slid open, revealing a man in a white lab coat. His mustache reminded me of Adolf Hitler's.

"Mrs. Clausen!" he said, extending his hand to Auntie Mildred. How he knew which one she was, I had no idea. "My name is Dr. Franks."

Auntie Mildred hesitated, then gently shook his hand.

Dr. Franks set his sights on Mama. "And you are . . . ?"

"Anna Higbee." She jerked a thumb over her shoulder. "But then, I'm surprised your interrogators didn't tell you."

Dr. Franks forced a nervous chuckle. "Yes, they are quite thorough. But the work we do here at Ingolstadt is of a very sensitive—"

"Nature," Mama finished. "They already mentioned that."

"I'm sure they did," he said, then bent down to look at me. He didn't have to bend far. "And what's your name, little missy?"

"Ella Mae," I said, catching a whiff of his cologne. He smelled like moldy pickles, which probably explained why his ring finger was bare.

Dr. Franks straightened back up. "Regrettably," he said to no one in particular, "I don't think our experiment is exactly appropriate for someone of Ella's age—"

"Ella *Mae*," I cut in.

Mama stuck out her chin. "If it ain't appropriate for my daughter, it ain't appropriate for us, either."

Dr. Franks didn't argue. "In that case," he replied, gesturing toward the screen (which turned out to be a window), "I invite you to witness the rebirth of subject oh-one-eight, otherwise known as Robert Clausen."

So that was it, the big secret? Dr. Franks really thought he could bring folks back to life? The last time I checked, only God could do that. I wanted to ask Mama what she thought of this tripe, but she just stood there staring, like she'd known all along.

The rectangular room on the other side of the window wasn't any bigger than this one. The only thing inside it was a giant red horse pill. A dark line ran down its middle, and on one side of the line, a screen winked on and off, like it was warming up.

The room certainly looked official, but it would take more than a few props to get me to change my mind. "If that's really Robby, how'd he get in there?"

Dr. Franks tilted his head. "Are you familiar with the birds and bees, Miss Higbee?"

"Who ain't familiar with birds and bees?" I replied at the same time Mama said "I beg your pardon!"

Luckily, Dr. Franks paid her no heed. "You see, Miss Higbee," he said, "every human life begins as a single fertilized egg. That egg contains forty-six chromosomes, which tell the embryo how it should grow. Once we had an egg, which we procured from a donor, all we had to do was strip it of its chromosomes—delete its identity, if you will—and reinsert the chromosomes we collected from your sample."

"What sample?" I asked.

Mama made a face. "He's talkin' about Robby's blood."

"Precisely," he said as he nodded toward the horse pill. "Then we placed the egg in that pod and waited for it to grow."

I didn't see what eggs or chromosomes had to do with birds or bees, but since Mama seemed to know, I decided I'd ask her later. I couldn't play detective if I looked uninformed. "So you're sayin' he'll be a baby when he comes out of that thing?"

Dr. Franks snorted. "Of course not. What use would a boy have for a baby's body? My pods are equipped with a gel that aids the growth *and* development of the fertilized egg.

In this way, I accomplish in a matter of months what it takes Mother Nature many years to achieve."

This might have sounded impressive, but I wasn't fooled. He'd probably made up half those words. But instead of engaging him in a big-words debate, I set my sights on the television. It said 29, then 28, then 27, counting down.

"What's gonna happen when it gets to zero?" I asked.

Dr. Franks smiled like the Cheshire cat. "Why, Robert Clausen will be reborn."

I still didn't believe a word of this nonsense, but Auntie Mildred fell for it hook, line, and sinker. The sheer force of his words seemed to knock her off balance, and she lunged for the window (or maybe the horse pill itself). Only her bony hands, which were clasped tightly in front of her, kept her from smashing into the glass.

"Careful," Mama said. "You know, maybe you shouldn't—"

"Hush," Auntie Mildred cut in. For once, she sounded like the strong one.

Mama clamped her lips shut, but the television kept going:

12.

11.

10.

"The subject may need some time," Dr. Franks said suddenly. "He probably won't remember everything all at once. I don't mean to alarm you, but the other subjects have struggled—which is to say that they haven't adapted as quickly as we'd like."

"Mildred," Mama whispered. "Are you absolutely certain that this is what you want?"

A single tear spilled down her cheek. "Yes, Anna, I'm sure."

3.

2.

1.

The line glowed, something hissed, and the horse pill split in half. Steam poured through the opening as a dim outline emerged.

I cupped my hands around my eyes and pressed my nose to the glass. As the shape took a wobbly step out of the horse pill, it resolved into a man. A man that might be Robby.

My heart sank to my toes. What if it really *was* Robby? What if he'd come back to life and the first face he saw was mine? It should have been Theo's or even Gracie's. Someone from his *real* family, not me.

Before I could retreat, the man bobbled and fell. Auntie Mildred gasped—she probably wanted to help him—but before she or Dr. Franks could rush to his aid, the man managed to drag himself back to his feet. When he looked up, our eyes met, and I saw three things all at once:

First, he was a man—or at least a boy—with arms and everything.

Second, he was naked.

And third, he wasn't Robby. He was Japanese.

Mama attempted to cover my eyes, but it was a halfhearted move, more thought than action. When I knocked her hand away, she didn't try to resist.

We stared at the man, and he stared back at us. I couldn't tell how old he was—I'd always been terrible at guessing ages at the county fair—but he looked as old as Robby when he left for the war. The fact that he was naked—and covered in slime—didn't seem to concern him. I couldn't help but be impressed.

Dr. Franks gasped. "What on earth . . . ?"

"Is this a joke?" Mama asked.

"Of course not," he replied, slithering backward a step.

The panic in his voice—and the look on Mama's face—made my hands start to sweat. I hadn't expected Robby to come out of that pod, but I certainly hadn't expected a Japanese man to, either.

"Would you care to explain where *he* came from?" she asked.

"How should I know?" he replied. "That was supposed to be Robert Clausen, not some baby-faced Jap!"

Auntie Mildred was too busy staring at a spot on the wall to do much more than blink, but I swallowed, hard. The Japanese had bombed Pearl Harbor when I was just a baby, but I knew why people hated them. Why they still called them names. The war they'd dragged us into had taken my cousin, Robby; my brother, Daniel; and at least one son or daughter from every family in St. Jude. Forgiving wasn't easy when you lost someone you loved.

Dr. Franks, who'd been backpedaling since the Japanese man had emerged, crashed into the door. "I don't understand." He grabbed a nearby clipboard. "The DNA's never wrong."

"What's DNA?" Mama asked.

"It's an abbreviation," he said as he fluttered through several pages. "It stands for deoxyribonucleic acid." He smacked the clipboard. "And it's never, ever wrong!"

"Then there must be some mistake." Mama pried the clipboard from his hands. "You cockamamie scientists must have more of these capsule things. Robby's probably in one of them."

His head bobbed up and down. "Well, yes, I suppose he could be. I need to check with Imogene." And with that, he seized the clipboard and scurried out of the room.

The soft snick of the door sliding shut on his heels was enough to snap Auntie Mildred out of her trance. She covered her face with her hands, and though she didn't make a sound, her bony shoulders shook from the violence of her sobs. I tried to feel what she was feeling, but the tremors wouldn't come. We'd buried Robby a long time ago. This loss felt small compared to that one.

While Mama tried to comfort Auntie Mildred, I sneaked another peek at the Japanese man. I'd been so certain that no one would come out of that horse pill, so now that someone had, I wanted to make sure he was real. His hair was black and caked with slime, which made it stick out every which way, but since it looked like a bird's nest, I decided I liked it. His eyes were dark brown and shaped like sideways teardrops.

I slid along the window until I was even with him. I'd seen his arms and legs, but maybe he had four thumbs or flippers instead of feet. There was only one way to find out. After drawing a deep breath, I pressed my hand to the glass.

He must have known what I wanted, because he took a shaky step toward me. His legs caved underneath him, but once he regained his balance, he pressed his hand to the glass, his left against my right. His hand was bigger than mine, but it *was* a hand, with four tapered fingers and one crooked thumb. Our palms didn't touch, but as slime outlined our hands, I thought I could feel the heat radiating off his skin.

Worry and excitement warred inside me, battling for my attention. But before one could win, Mama barked, "What are you doin'? Take your hand down from there, and turn around this instant. If your daddy only knew what you were lookin' at . . ."

Grudgingly, I dropped my hand, but I stayed where I was. The Japanese man was a mystery I intended to solve.

For all of his so-called intelligence, Dr. Franks had no idea where the Japanese man had come from. As far as their records indicated (and their records were *very accurate*, he assured us), they'd injected the donated egg with Auntie Mildred's sample. He only had one explanation for why it hadn't grown into my cousin: the DNA—the blood—on my cousin's dog tags must not have belonged to him.

Mama made a face. "That ain't an explanation," she said.

"Well, it's the best one I've got. The science is still quite new. That's why we call it a test."

Mama didn't try to reason with Dr. Franks, just grabbed her sister's arm. "Let's go," she mumbled.

Dr. Franks lowered his clipboard. "But aren't you going to take him?" He motioned toward the window.

"Take him *where*?" Mama asked.

Dr. Franks blinked. "Home, of course."

Auntie Mildred's eyes fluttered, which was what they always did when she started to swoon. We had to do something, and fast. Mama smacked her cheek while I kicked her in the shins. The kicking was usually Gracie's job, but I'd seen her do it plenty of times.

Auntie Mildred straightened back up. "Thank you," she peeped.

"My pleasure," I said.

Mama returned her attention to Dr. Franks. "Did you really think we would just take him home?"

"Well, yes," he replied. "Ingolstadt's not equipped to house our subjects on a long-term basis. This is a laboratory, not the Biltmore."

I wished it *were* the Biltmore. Then it would have had room service—not to mention a pool—instead of these tiny rooms and the lingering aroma of Dr. Franks's cologne.

Mama tried a new tack. "What about your research?"

"Oh, well, you'll bring him back every week for the next couple of months."

Mama snorted. "Not likely."

Dr. Franks sputtered. "But Mrs. Clausen signed a contract! She agreed to take custody."

"No," Mama said, "she agreed to take Robby."

Mama rushed us away without a backward glance. I dragged my feet, wanting to catch one last glimpse of the Japanese man, but Mama's grip was as tight as Uncle George's bear traps. Dr. Franks pursued us, but Mama ignored his fervent pleas, her mouth set in a grim line.

We took several wrong turns, but Mama never wavered. When we finally emerged into the lobby with the three-story portrait, it was by the sheer force of her will. The secretary refused to meet our eyes as we skittered out the mouth door, which zoomed shut on our heels like it was spitting us out.

It wasn't until the afternoon sun started to thaw out my

arms that I realized how cold I was, and suddenly, I felt a little sorry for the Japanese man. Would he ever know the feeling of sunshine on prickly goose bumps, or of fresh air in cooped-up lungs?

Auntie Mildred shook her head as we climbed into the car. "I can't take him. I won't. I told them I'd take Robby, not this . . . this *imposter.*"

Mama jerked the gearshift into reverse. "Didn't I say that ad was trouble?"

"I just wanted Robby back." Auntie Mildred's shoulders slumped. "Dr. Franks said they'd discovered the secret of life."

Mama's nose wrinkled. "He ain't God Himself."

"He sounded smart," she went on. "He knew stuff we didn't."

"Lots of folks know stuff we don't, but that doesn't make 'em smart."

Mama and Auntie Mildred didn't say another word for the rest of the ride, though I would have welcomed the entertainment. The drive was as dull as Mama's silver, nothing but rolling hills and clumps of sage for as far as the eye could see. Or maybe it wasn't the drive that was really the problem. My thoughts were tangled knots that I couldn't untie, but I wasn't sure if I wanted to. The others seemed to think that the Japanese man was a criminal, but how could you decide if a man was good or bad just by looking at his face?

I was still trying to decide when we turned off the old

highway, but before I could ask, Auntie Mildred finally cracked.

"I've been thinking," she said. "There's only one way that blood could have ended up on those dog tags."

Auntie Mildred gave us a chance to work it out on our own, but me and Mama were less thinkers, more doers. We didn't work anything out before her patience ran dry.

"There must have been some sort of scuffle." Auntie Mildred hissed the words as she leaned across the seat. "Then he must have killed my son."

I might not have had the brains to come up with the answer on my own, but I could spot the truth when someone pointed me in its direction. Worry rumbled in my stomach like a pack of restless squirrels. If the Japanese man had killed Robby, would he kill us, too? I glanced at Mama to see if she'd had the same thought, but her face in the rearview was a blank mask.

"That's quite an accusation," she said.

Auntie Mildred sniffed. "It'll turn out to be true. You just wait and see."

3

Daddy didn't get home that night until it was almost time for dinner. As soon as he walked through the door, he hung his hat on the coatrack and retrieved his dinner jacket. He always wore it to eat, just like he never left home without a hat on his head. I figured that was why they called it a dinner jacket.

"Evening, Anna," he said as he strolled into the kitchen.

She looked up from the ham she'd been dragging out of the oven. "I'm sorry we're late. It's been one of those days."

"Tell me about it," he said, relieving her of the ham. He set it on the table with an audible thunk. "But really, I don't mind."

Mama kissed him soundly. "I appreciate your assistance."

Daddy grinned. "My pleasure."

I pretended to hurl into the mashed potatoes, but neither of them seemed to notice.

Eventually, Mama returned her attention to the ham. "Did you have a nice time at the pier?"

"Not really," he said. "For some reason I can't quite fathom, the fish prefer George's line." He sneaked a piece of ham. "Did you have a nice time baking cookies?"

"Actually," I replied, "we didn't have time to make cookies. Auntie Mildred called after lunch, and we had to—"

"Ella Mae," Mama said, "how are those potatoes lookin'?"

I inspected my handiwork. I could have made a stink that she hadn't let me finish, but I'd long since figured out that mamas played by different rules. "I'd say they're lookin' mashed."

Mama untied her apron. "Then I'd say it's time to eat."

I set the potatoes down next to the ham, then squeezed into my seat. Daniel's was more accessible, but no one sat in Daniel's chair. If we had dinner guests, Mama made us eat outside. Other folks might have minded, but it made sense to me. I wanted Daniel to come home and take his seat at the table almost as much as she did.

Daddy held out his hands. His prayers were short and sweet, but that was just the way I liked them. I figured Jesus liked them that way, too, since He had to listen to so many.

After he finished the prayer, Mama dished up the potatoes. They only looked slightly lumpy. "I assume you ate the fish for lunch?"

Daddy nodded. "You know George."

Uncle George had been an Eagle Scout since they were first invented, so he didn't believe in frying fish in pans. Instead of bringing his catch home, he roasted it right there on the beach, where it would taste like sand and surf. Since

Auntie Mildred only cooked what Betty Crocker told her to, this arrangement worked out well.

Mama took a sip of sweet tea. "I guess buying that electric range was a waste of money."

"It does match their Chrysler," Daddy said.

"And their toaster," I replied.

"They make teal toasters?" Daddy asked.

Mama scooped up some green beans. "They make teal *everything*."

"Including houses," I said.

Mama shook her head. "No, that's completely different." She scooped up some more green beans (though I knew for a fact that she only ate green beans because they were good for you). "Our house is sky blue, not teal."

Our house was certainly *something*. It used to be white, but on the one-year anniversary of my brother's death, Mama had decided that white was too drab. It had taken her a few weeks to pick out a new color, but once she'd settled on blue, it had only taken us a few days to paint it. Slow to judge, quick to act—that was how Mama lived.

Daddy raised his glass. "Well, thank goodness I married the sensible Simpson."

Mama clinked her glass to his. "You can put that on my tombstone."

He speared a slice of ham. "Everything's delicious, sweetheart. You two must have spent the whole day in the kitchen."

"Actually," I said, "we didn't get back until—"

I broke off when something—or someone—kicked me in the shins.

Mama smiled sweetly. "Pass the butter, will you, sweetness?"

Scowling, I passed the butter. I would have made more of a fuss, but I didn't fancy getting kicked again.

Daddy speared another slice of ham. "Where did you go?" he asked.

When Mama didn't answer right away, I took advantage of her silence: "We drove up to Pasadena to meet a man named Dr. Franks. He grows folks in these red horse pills, and one of them should have been Robby, but he was Japanese instead."

I'd tucked my legs under my chair about halfway through this speech, but I needn't have bothered. Mama's attention was on Daddy, who arched an eyebrow at her. When Mama shook her head, Daddy burst into guffaws.

"What's so funny?" I demanded. I really didn't like being the only person in the family under the age of forty-five. It made it hard to get the jokes.

"You are," Daddy said.

I knotted my arms across my waist. "I was tryin' to be serious."

"We *know*," Mama replied as she nudged me with her foot.

The emphasis she put on that one word said more than ten or twenty could have, but Daddy didn't seem to notice.

"Maybe we ought to take a break from Sergeant Friday,"

he said, winking. "I didn't realize you had such a vivid imagination."

He and Mama went on laughing like a pair of drunken sailors, but I didn't join in. No matter what people said, most folks laughed *at* you, not with you. I drained my milk in one swallow, then slammed the glass down on the table (since that was what the cowboys in all of Daddy's Westerns did).

"May I be excused?"

At least that got their attention. "Aren't you hungry?" Daddy asked.

Irritably, I shook my head. "Seeing men come back to life kind of takes away your appetite."

Daddy's forehead wrinkled, but before he had a chance to ask me what I meant, Mama said, "I'm sorry you're not feelin' well. Maybe you should go upstairs."

She meant that I should go upstairs before I spilled the beans, but I'd already spilled them, and Daddy still hadn't believed me. We'd been partners in crime since Daniel had left for the war, so this brush-off was especially painful. I set my plate down in the sink, then headed upstairs to my room.

I stormed past Daniel's door, which was closed like always, the doorjambs standing guard like a pair of silent soldiers. Mama kept his room exactly as he'd left it, as if he might come home someday and pick up the pieces of his life. I couldn't say I blamed her. Daniel was the only thing she'd brought all the way from Alabama after the Depression and the Dust Bowl had forced them to head west. She'd always called Daniel her home's blood and me her little miracle, but maybe if she'd called Daniel the same thing, he wouldn't have stepped on that land mine.

I flopped down on my bed and tucked my hands behind my head. Normally, I liked making sense out of the squiggles on my ceiling, but today, they looked like twisty halls and horse pills filled with men.

I rolled onto my side. "I thought God was the only one who could bring folks back to life, but it looks like Dr. Franks can, too," I whispered to the yellow wall that I'd once shared with Daniel. But I couldn't bring myself to ask the question in my head: *If God let Dr. Franks resurrect a Japanese man, why couldn't He let Dr. Franks resurrect you, too?*

4

Mama might have kept me from telling Daddy the whole truth, but there was nothing she could do to keep me from telling Theo. We'd been nearly inseparable since Mama and Auntie Mildred had popped us out in the same week, and the only way that Mama could stop us from seeing each other would be to keep me home from Sunday school (which we both knew she wouldn't do).

But when I made it to the church bright and early Sunday morning, Theo was nowhere to be found. I even waited in our usual spot underneath the choir seats for an extra fifteen minutes (and I would have waited longer if it hadn't been for Mrs. Timothy). I had to endure another lesson about fire and brimstone by myself, but as soon as the bell rang, I escaped into the hall.

It didn't take me long to find him, since I knew all of Theo's haunts. After checking underneath the choir seats again, I slipped out the side door and inspected every shrub around the old adobe church. Sure enough, I found him and Walter tucked behind the biggest bush.

"Hey, watch it!" Walter said when I almost tripped over his shoes.

"Oh, don't be such a baby. I bet you don't even polish 'em." I flicked Theo's ear. "What are you doin' with this lamebrain?"

"For your information," Walter said, "Theo and I are in the middle of a very important business deal."

That business deal looked like a rip-roaring game of marbles. And judging by the heap of steelies Walter had amassed, it looked like they weren't messing around.

I stuck both hands on my hips. "Theodore Clausen, are you gamblin' on the Lord's own doorstep?"

Walter smiled smugly. "You can't really call it gambling if you know you're going to lose."

Theo dropped his gaze. Dark curls spilled across his forehead, obscuring the thin scar he'd received when I accidentally launched a firework at him.

"I ought to hand you over to your mama"—I plopped down in the dirt—"for not inviting me."

A tiny smile tugged at one corner of his mouth, but he didn't look up.

Walter scooted back. "Hey, who said you could stay?"

"I did," I replied, seizing one of his clearies and holding it up to the light. It was bright enough to make me squint. "If you don't want me to squeal, you're gonna have to pay me off."

Walter made a face. "Why, you little—"

"Careful," I said. "You wouldn't want the angels recordin' any of your filthy words."

It looked like he dearly wanted to wrap his hands around my neck, but instead of working up the nerve, he knotted his arms across his chest. He might have gambled on the Lord's own doorstep, but apparently, he drew the line at murder. Guess even Walter Lloyd had standards.

"I'll take this clearie for my silence." I stuck it in my pocket without waiting for his say-so. "And I want Theo's marbles back."

Walter's face flushed purple. "Why don't you take them all?" he asked as he kicked the heap at Theo. As he stalked away, he added, "I'll just win them back next week."

I glared at Walter's back until he disappeared around the corner, then retrieved one of his shooters. It was as heavy as a ball of lead. "What were you thinkin', Theo? Everyone knows that Walter cheats."

He swiped the shooter from my hand. "I was thinkin' I was tired of listenin' to Mrs. Timothy."

I flicked his ear again. "I would've played with you."

"Yeah, well, you were late."

"Well, then, you should have waited!"

Theo clambered to his feet. "I don't need your lectures." He dusted off his pants and headed toward the parking lot. "And I certainly don't need you fightin' my battles for me."

"Well, sor-ree," I said as I hurried to keep up. "If I'd known you were gonna be so cranky, I wouldn't have bothered to come and tell you about the lab."

"What lab?" Theo asked.

He said it like he didn't think there really was a lab, like he was trying to be nice, but then, Theo had never had a very good imagination. I blamed that on Auntie Mildred.

"The lab that me and Mama drove your mama to," I said as I sidled up to him. "Want to guess what happened when we got there?"

"Not really," Theo said.

"We saw a man come back to life!" I cupped a hand around my mouth. "And not just any man," I whispered, "but a real, live Japanese—"

I broke off when we ran smack-dab into Walter, who was skulking around the palm trees that lined the front of the church.

I shoved him in the back. "Criminy, Walter!"

He clamped a hand over my mouth. "Quiet, Ella Mae. Do you want someone to see us?"

Did I want someone to see Walter's hand touching my lips? Absolutely not.

Once he was sure I wouldn't squeal, Walter dropped his hand and nodded toward Mr. and Mrs. Dent, who were saying good-bye to Reverend Simms. "I'm just trying to avoid the Dirts."

Hearing Walter say that left a bad taste in my mouth. The whole town had turned out for the Dents' after-the-war wedding, but Mama said the only reason that anyone had gone was to gawk at the Hawaiian bride. At the party afterward, I'd heard Auntie Mildred say, "White men and brown women weren't meant to live together. A bird might love a fish, but where on earth would they keep house?"

But as far as I could tell, the Dents were doing just fine. They had two kids, a steady income, and a bungalow on Finch Street. Walter and Auntie Mildred were the ones who had the problem.

I rubbed the goose bumps on my arms and looked around for an escape route, but there was no way to avoid the scene playing out on the church steps. I watched reluctantly as Mrs. Dent held out her hand and Reverend Simms shook it, but as soon as the Dents turned around, he wiped his hand off on his pants.

"Did you see that?" Walter hissed. "The reverend doesn't like those Dirts, either."

"Pipe down," I said so softly he probably couldn't even hear. I considered it my duty to put Walter in his place, but I'd never seen him and Reverend Simms agree on *anything* important. Whether that made it more right or more wrong, though, I couldn't have said.

Once the Dents got in their car, Walter dusted off his hands. "Looks like it's finally safe." He gave me and Theo a two-fingered salute. "I guess I'll see you around."

We didn't return his salute, just watched him go through squinted eyes. Walter always made me mad, but today, he'd made me nervous, too. If that was how people reacted to a perfectly nice Hawaiian lady, how in the world would they respond to a full-blown Japanese man?

Once Walter left, Theo set his sights on me. "Weren't you gonna tell me something?"

I rolled my tongue around my mouth (which still tasted horrible). "No, it ain't important."

Suddenly, the thought of telling Theo—and having him react like Walter—made me want to retreat into my shell and never poke my head back out. There was no guarantee that he'd fly off the handle, but what if he did? I didn't want to take the risk.

5

Thursday night found me and Daddy watching *Dragnet* in the living room. Daddy might have thought that teal toasters were stupid, but as soon as Mr. Leavitt had introduced him to the television, that was all she wrote. Daddy said it reminded him of listening to the radio with Gramps, but Mama called the television "the demise of imagination."

I tuned in to NBC while Daddy got settled in his armchair. Daniel used to be the official tuner in the family, but after the war ended, Daddy gave me the job. He said he'd just been waiting for my fingers to get strong enough, but I knew he'd been hoping that Daniel would come home. I'd been hoping that, too.

Mama poked her head in as the picture glowed to life. "Is *I Love Lucy* on?"

I crinkled my nose. "*I Love Lucy* is on Mondays. It's *Dragnet* tonight."

Mama grunted. "Really, Jed? I thought we both agreed that Ella Mae's too sensitive."

"You think everyone's too sensitive," I said as I spread out on the rug.

Daddy held up his hands. "One more episode won't hurt."

Mama rolled her eyes. "At least sit on the couch!" she hollered at me over her shoulder. "You're too old to let folks get a look at your bloomers."

With a heavy sigh, I retreated to the couch, one of Auntie Mildred's lumpy hand-me-downs. Sergeant Friday's badge flashed across the screen, and then his voice boomed through the living room: "The story you are about to see is true. The names have been changed to protect the innocent." I tried to focus on his monologue about the evening's case, but the words got mixed up in my brain. I must have been too busy being sensitive about being sensitive.

"You can stop pouting," Daddy said when the show cut to commercials. "She said you could watch."

"I'm too old for fishin' and for lyin' on the floor. Now I'm too sensitive for *Dragnet*?"

"She didn't mean it like that, Ella Mae."

I glowered. "Yes, she did."

He didn't disagree.

"I didn't make it up, you know. I really saw a Japanese man."

"I'm sure you did," Daddy said.

"So why don't you believe me?"

Daddy shifted awkwardly. "I believe that you believe. Isn't that enough?"

"No," I said, "it ain't."

The advertisements ended, and so did our conversation. I'd learned months ago not to interrupt the sergeant. But

33

just because I couldn't say the words out loud didn't make them go away. They swam around inside my head like a school of restless salmon, too slippery to catch but too tickly to ignore.

Friday afternoon found me and Theo walking home from school together. I still hadn't told him about the Japanese man, even though we walked home every day (except when it was raining). I liked these days best, when the air was warm but not hot, dry but not dusty. We were still several blocks from home, but I could already smell Mr. McConnell's orange grove.

"Did you see Rusty's hair?" I asked. "It looked like someone slathered a pound of Brylcreem on his head."

"Oh, was that Brylcreem?" Theo shuddered. "It looked like slime to me."

That made me think of the Japanese man, and *that* made me shudder involuntarily, too. I was trying to decide if keeping him a secret was still the best course of action when a bicycle bell dinged behind us. I didn't have to turn around to know that it was Gracie.

"Theo!" she yelled. "Ella Mae! I need to talk to you!"

We exchanged a solemn look, then, by unspoken agreement, turned around. We could have outrun her if she'd been on foot, but we were no match for Gracie's bicycle. Mama had once offered to teach her how to drive, but after Auntie Mildred argued, loudly, Gracie had assured us that she preferred to ride. Auntie Mildred wasn't fond of Gracie's bicycle, either, but apparently, riding bicycles was more ladylike than driving cars.

Gracie was breathing hard as she rolled to a stop. "Mama wanted me to tell you that she's almost out of jam, so if Auntie Anna has leftovers, Mama would appreciate a loan."

Auntie Mildred's orange marmalade had always been my favorite, but when she sold her soul to Betty Crocker, she'd also given up canning. Now we were stuck with Mama's strawberry, which tasted just fine if you could get past all the seeds.

"I'll pass the word along," I said.

Gracie set her sights on Theo. "And she asked me to remind you about your dentist's appointment. You've got to leave for Santa Ana in the next twenty-five minutes."

Theo made a face. "I was hopin' she'd forget."

"Fat chance," I replied as I nudged him with my elbow. "Auntie Mildred never forgets *anything*."

"Tell me about it," Theo said.

We were still just standing there, not leaving, when Theo dragged a hand under his nose. His elbow swung so wide that it whacked me in the shoulder.

I grabbed my arm. "Hey, watch it!"

Theo didn't apologize, though his eyes did widen. We'd been cousins long enough that I knew exactly what he meant.

"I mean," I said, dropping my hand, "Theo can't go to the dentist because he already promised that he'd help me with my times tables."

Gracie arched an eyebrow. I was usually much better at lying; she'd just caught me off guard. But before I could lay the grease on even thicker, Gracie said, "All right."

Theo sagged with relief.

"But I'm coming with you," she went on after glancing at her watch. "When Theo has to go, I'll help you finish up."

I started to protest, but Theo elbowed me again. Reluctantly, I shut my trap. He'd always been a pacifist, and heaven forbid that I should fight his battles for him.

Gracie trailed along behind us for the last couple of blocks, dipping her head at Mrs. Olsen and blushing when Patrick Temple winked at her from the other side of the street. By the time we made it to our picket fence, Mr. McConnell's orange blossoms didn't smell nearly as sweet.

I yanked Theo through the gate. "We'll only be a second!" I hollered back at Gracie. With any luck, another boy would pedal down the street, and she'd lose track of the time.

But it didn't look like Gracie was in the mood to be side-tracked. "I'll be right behind you," she replied, leaning her bicycle against the fence.

I hustled him into the house. If Gracie expected me to hold the door open for her, she had another thing coming. I wasn't one of her lovesick lackeys. We tumbled into the kitchen, where Mama was on the telephone.

"—speakin' to her," she was saying, twisting the cord around her hand, adding curlicues to curlicues. But then her hand went still. "How did you get this number?"

The chilliness in Mama's voice made me miss a step.

"Well, of course she did," Mama said, "but that doesn't mean I've taken charge of anything!"

I suspected the *she* was Auntie Mildred, but I couldn't have said for sure. As we edged closer to Mama, Theo's shoe squeaked on the linoleum, and Mama whirled around. Her eyes bulged when she spotted him.

"Get him out of here!" she roared. She'd pressed a hand over the mouthpiece, but it probably hadn't done much good.

Stunned, I staggered back, dragging Theo with me. The last time I'd heard Mama roar like that, she'd just found out that Daniel wouldn't be coming home. We crashed into Gracie as we stumbled onto the porch, but Mama didn't stop herding us. Once our toes were clear of the door, she slammed it shut in our faces.

"What's her problem?" Theo asked.

I made a show of shrugging. Her reaction had affected me, but I wasn't about to let it show. "I think she just needs a nap."

Gracie saw through my nonchalance. "Is there something we can do?"

"Oh, I think you've done enough." The sooner I got rid of Gracie and her well-intentioned meddling, the sooner I could find out what was going on. "Thanks for comin' over."

Gracie grabbed the railing. "But what about your times tables?"

"I can do 'em on my own." I couldn't bring myself to look at Theo. "Hope the dentist doesn't kill you."

He knotted his arms across his chest. "It'll be your fault if he does."

Gracie only made it halfway down the walk before she realized he wasn't with her. "Theo, are you coming?"

"Yeah, I'll be right there." But as soon as Gracie turned around, he turned back to me. "Ella Mae, what's goin' on? Who was your mama talkin' to?"

I opened my mouth to answer, then snapped it shut again. "I don't know," I admitted, and it was even mostly true.

"Come on," Theo said, dropping his voice. "You can lie to Gracie, but you can't lie to me."

"It's true," I said, because it was. When he still just stood there waiting, I shoved him down the stairs. If I'd gone this long without telling him about the Japanese man, I could go a little longer. "Don't want to keep the dentist waiting."

He didn't look like he believed me, but I didn't give him time to argue, just hurried back inside. I was itching to hear what they were saying, but Mama had already hung up (though the cord hadn't stopped swinging).

"Who was that?" I asked.

"It was Miss Kendall," Mama said, "Dr. Franks's secretary. She said they want us to come back."

I sneered. "Of course they do."

Mama's fingers curled around the counter. "I told her we would."

"But why?" I asked, dumbfounded.

"She said they've had some sort of breakthrough." Mama drew a shaky breath. "Not that she would tell me what the breakthrough *was*, but she made it sound like they found Robby."

6

We picked up Auntie Mildred first thing Saturday morning. She was waiting for us on her porch, clutching her purse like a life preserver. The rain dripping from the eaves softened her rough edges.

"This is it," she said as she climbed into our Studebaker. "I can feel it."

I didn't bother to point out that she'd probably thought the same thing last week.

It took longer than it should have to reach the old highway. The rain turned the landscape gray and drizzly, reducing the San Bernardinos to distant blobs and muffling all but the hypnotic swishing of our tires on the wet road. Mama hated driving slow, but she must have hated the thought of wrecking Daddy's Studebaker even more. When we pulled into the parking lot of Ingolstadt Laboratories, we were fifteen minutes late.

Auntie Mildred didn't wait for Mama to turn off the engine, just jumped out of the car as soon as it rolled to a stop (or maybe slightly before). When I didn't go as fast as she wanted me to, Auntie Mildred grabbed my wrist and towed me into the lobby. Her gloves felt slick, like sweaty hands.

The secretary beamed at our approach. "What can I do for you?" she asked as we scurried across the shiny tiles. She wasn't the same secretary who'd been here the week before.

Auntie Mildred licked her lips. "We're here to talk to Dr. Franks."

The secretary consulted her appointment book. "Oh, you must be Mrs. Higbee."

"Actually, I'm Mrs. Clausen."

"Oh, yes, Mrs. Clausen. I have your name right here." The secretary bit her lip. "Now, as I'm sure you've guessed, I'm going to need to see ID."

Mama produced her driver's license while Auntie Mildred fumbled for her water bill. I caught a glimpse of the postmark as she passed it to the secretary, but neither of them seemed to notice it was more than a month old. I kept that tidbit to myself. If Auntie Mildred's ID was no good, they might not let us past the guards, and I might never solve the mystery of the Japanese man.

We only made it past four checkpoints before Dr. Franks appeared. His lab coat looked as if he'd slept in it, but he was grinning like an idiot. I definitely wouldn't be grinning if I had to try to sleep in this awful, freezing place.

"Mrs. Higbee," he said, "you came!"

Mama's eyes narrowed. "Did you think we wouldn't?"

Dr. Franks lowered his gaze. "I suppose I had my doubts. But I do think you'll appreciate what we've accomplished."

He directed us into a nearby elevator. "There's something I'd like to show you."

Auntie Mildred hurried aboard, eager to meet the breakthrough, but I lingered on the threshold, suddenly nervous. Something about the way that he'd lowered his eyes had made my stomach clench. What if this so-called accomplishment had nothing to do with Robby? What if we'd come all this way so Dr. Franks could show us his earwax collection?

The door tried to close on Auntie Mildred's heels, but Dr. Franks stopped it. "Were you planning to join us?"

Mama took my hand. "Courage, sweetness," she whispered as we stepped into the elevator.

The room he took us to was unlike any of the others we'd been in so far. For one thing, it was long, with two rows of theater seats that faced a large window, and for another, it was crammed. Two gray-colored folks were standing closest to the door. Their eyes and cheeks were sunken, as if they hadn't slept in weeks. A frantic-looking mama with a pack of squabbling kids was standing next to them, and farther down, an old man with a leathery face couldn't seem to stop frowning. There were other folks, too, but those four stood out. They looked like they needed a hug.

"Who are they?" I asked as Auntie Mildred elbowed around them.

"The other families, of course." Dr. Franks motioned toward the window. "They're here to see the demonstration."

Mama's forehead wrinkled. "But why are they interested in Robby?"

Dr. Franks leaned toward her. "Come again?"

"I said, why are they interested in Robby?"

Instead of waiting to hear his answer, I dove into the crowd behind Auntie Mildred. The other families had cleared a path, and it still hadn't filled in. They must have been wary of her pointy elbows.

"Where is he?" she mumbled.

I pressed my nose against the window. It looked down on a gym with a balance beam, monkey bars, and a set of mini hurdles. Several dozen assistants were fluttering around the subjects, whose teal robes and bare feet made them easy to spot. It seemed like Dr. Franks could have at least found them some socks. There were few things I hated more than cold feet.

Auntie Mildred bent this way and that as she inspected the subjects. "Where *is* he? I can't see him."

But I could see the Japanese man. His teal robe and bare feet couldn't hide his black hair. Someone had tried to tame it, but it still stuck out every which way. They'd tucked him into a corner, obviously apart from the rest, who were sitting in hard plastic chairs (or, in some cases, slouching).

Auntie Mildred trembled. "He isn't here," she whispered, then shouted it again: "Anna, he isn't here!"

The other families, who'd been chatting quietly, snapped to attention. Their eyes settled on Auntie Mildred (whose eyes were filling with tears).

Dr. Franks perked up. "*Who* isn't?"

"Who do you think?" Mama asked.

When Dr. Franks didn't answer, I rolled my eyes. "They're talkin' about Robby," I said.

Dr. Franks's forehead crinkled. "Why would he be?" he asked. He seemed genuinely confused.

"Because you found him," I replied. "You said you had a breakthrough."

"We *did* have a breakthrough," he said, "but we have not found Robert Clausen."

I swallowed, hard. I'd suspected as much, but it was still hard to hear. Mama's hands clenched into fists, though she managed not to swing them. Auntie Mildred didn't react— on the outside, at least. I could only imagine what was going on under that pale pink hat.

"My apologies," he went on after clearing his throat. When we just stood there, stunned, he pressed a nearby button, and an intercom crackled to life. "You can go ahead, Jackson."

As Dr. Franks's words reverberated around the gym, the assistants leaped to their feet. They grabbed the subjects— by their hands or their armpits, whichever was more conve- nient—and dragged them from their seats. As I watched the subjects shuffle from one spot to another, I matched them to their families. The gray-colored man was probably the gray-colored people's son, and the girl with the frown had to belong to the old man. None of the subjects looked like the frantic-looking mama, but I decided she went with the tall man by the door. He was still just sitting there drooling, but she hadn't stopped staring the whole time we'd been here.

By contrast, the Japanese man belonged to no one. The assistants mostly ignored him, but he seemed fine on his own. He walked effortlessly to the balance beam and traversed it with ease. I'd tried my hand at walking plenty of fence rails in my day, but I always fell off. The Japanese man, on the other hand, didn't so much as bobble.

"You see?" Dr. Franks asked. "He's a breakthrough, a real breakthrough!"

I couldn't decide if he was a breakthrough or not, but he did look more stable than the other subjects, who were in various states of not-standing. When the Japanese man reached the end, he hopped off like a sparrow, then looked around to see if anyone had noticed. But the assistants were so busy getting drooled on—or worse—that none of them had.

The Japanese man eyed the others with something like curiosity. I couldn't say I blamed him. They were acting like a pack of overgrown toddlers, but instead of running for cover (like I would have, no doubt), the Japanese man turned around.

Dr. Franks tensed. "What's he doing?"

It hit me as soon as he reached another subject, a short, stocky woman who was on her hands and knees. "He wants to help," I whispered.

Sure enough, the Japanese man took one look at the woman, then extended a hand.

44

Before she could decide if she wanted to take it, Dr. Franks pounced on the intercom. "Keep him moving, Jackson! He must complete the whole course if we want to be able to make a full analysis."

"Are you talking about the Jap?" someone asked. "How'd he get here, anyway? And why's he not crawling like Maisie?"

Before Dr. Franks had a chance to answer, Auntie Mildred exploded. "He's an imposter!" she screamed. "And he was supposed to be *mine*!"

She thumped on the window, then crumpled into a ball. A growl started rumbling in her chest, then steadily built into a howl. It reminded me of the coyotes that roamed the hills during the night. When she dragged her nails along the glass, leaving inch-long scratches, the other families shifted back. I would have done the same if she hadn't been my flesh and blood.

It seemed like I should say something, since I was closer than Mama, but the sound she was making didn't promote conversation. I was about to chicken out when I remembered the Japanese man. If he could hold out a hand to a perfect stranger, then I could comfort my own auntie. Tentatively, I patted her shoulder, but as soon as I made contact, she yelped like a hurt dog and knocked my hand away. When it hit the window, it echoed like a gong—or a gunshot.

I was too stunned to do much more than stare, but Dr. Franks pounced on another button. "Imogene, I need backup! I repeat, I need backup!"

45

It only took a minute for the men in black suits to show up. While the other families crouched down and tried to make themselves less noticeable, the men dragged Auntie Mildred away from the window, then uncapped a needle and jammed it into her arm. It only took a second for Auntie Mildred's eyes to roll back in her head.

Mama's eyes hardened. "What have you done?" she demanded as they towed Auntie Mildred away. Her heels dragged on the tiles, leaving long black skid marks that would probably take days to scrub off.

I just stared at the spot where Auntie Mildred had fallen, trying to ignore the rising tide of nausea that was taking over my stomach. She'd never been my favorite relative, but watching those men jab her had rearranged my loyalties.

Dr. Franks held up his hands. "It was just a precaution," he said as he shrank away from Mama. "She was a danger to herself and others."

"She might have been a danger to that window, but she wasn't a danger to *you*." Mama tightened her grip on her purse. "You'll take me to her this instant, and then we're gonna leave."

Dr. Franks swallowed. "Very well."

When Mama seized my hand, I didn't even protest, just let her drag me out the door. The other families watched us go without saying a word. One man clenched his fists, but the frantic-looking mama waved him off. She must have refereed plenty of fights.

Auntie Mildred had ended up down the hall in a room

that looked like it had once been a closet. They'd taken out most of the shelves and replaced them with a metal table and two spindly chairs. By the time we arrived in the doorway, she was already coming to.

Mama breezed past the man silently guarding the door. I couldn't resist stepping on his giant black shoe, but the man didn't budge.

Mama knelt down by the chair they'd stuck Auntie Mildred in. "How are you feelin'?" Mama asked.

Auntie Mildred clutched her forehead. "Like someone cracked me with a shovel."

Mama pursed her lips. "Do you think you can stand?"

Auntie Mildred gripped the table and dragged herself back to her feet. She bobbled like a newborn calf, but somehow, she didn't fall. I couldn't help but be reminded of the Japanese man downstairs.

"Well, then," Mama said, "we'll just be on our way."

Dr. Franks fiddled with his sleeve. "A thousand apologies, Mrs. Clausen. What a terrible misunderstanding."

Auntie Mildred shrugged. *You didn't bring Robby back,* her thin shoulders seemed to say, *so I don't care anymore.*

Once we were safely in the elevator, I tugged on Mama's hand. "I take it we're not comin' back?"

"Oh, we're comin' back," Mama said, patting Auntie Mildred's hand. "Someone's got to teach that man that he can't treat folks like cattle." Under her breath, she added, "Not even Japanese ones."

Dr. Franks wasn't the only one who treated folks like cattle. Miss Fightmaster, my teacher, was fond of teaching boring lessons, then jabbing people with her ruler if they dared to interrupt.

I really didn't like that ruler, but when she stuffed our heads with fractions and more useless mumbo jumbo, I couldn't help but misbehave. At least Monday morning's lesson looked more promising than most. She scratched it on the board as soon as we walked through the door: "How the Mighty Oak Tree Grows from a Single Acorn."

"It might not look like it," she said as she handed out acorns (and hammers), "but this tiny seed is one of God's greatest creations. Add a little water and sunlight, and it will grow into a giant."

I held up my acorn. "Sounds like oak trees are a lot like people."

"Ella Mae, don't hold that acorn right in front of your nose! You'll make yourself go cross-eyed!" She whacked my desk with her ruler. "And you *must* raise your hand if you want my attention."

Grudgingly, I lowered my acorn, then stuck my hand in the air.

She let me stew for five whole seconds. "Yes, Ella Mae?"

I held up my acorn. "Sounds like oak trees are a lot like people."

This time, she ignored my deliberate attempt to make myself go cross-eyed. "I don't know what you mean."

"Well, you know how we come from eggs."

Behind me, someone laughed. "We're not chickens, Ella Mae!" It sounded suspiciously like Walter.

"I never said we were chickens." I flipped a braid over my shoulder. "I was just talkin' to this scientist, and *he* said that people—"

"Where did you meet a scientist, on a funny farm?"

Red-hot shame crept up my neck and set my ears on fire, but before I could whip around and introduce Walter to my fist, Miss Fightmaster intervened.

"Why don't we move on?" she asked, though it sounded less like a suggestion and more like a command.

"But I have a question," I said.

Miss Fightmaster smoothed her eyebrows. "All right, then, let's have it."

"Do these acorns have DNA?"

Now, I wasn't above dragging out a conversation to waste time, but in the case of these acorns, I genuinely wanted to know.

Miss Fightmaster pressed her lips into a line. "I'm afraid I'm not familiar with that term."

"I'm not familiar with it, either," I said, "but I think it stands for deoxyribo-something-or-other. Dr. Franks said it's in everything, which is what made me wonder if it's in these acorns, too."

Her nostrils shriveled into slits. "There will be no more talk of scientists." She jabbed me with her ruler. "And there will be no more talk of DNA, either."

Miss Fightmaster continued, but I was no longer listening. How *did* these acorns know how to grow into oak trees? Why didn't they ever grow into beech trees instead?

"I think these little acorns must have DNA," I said. "God probably invented it to keep everything straight."

This time, Miss Fightmaster's entire face shriveled. She swept my acorn onto the floor and ground it to dust with her heel. "This class will not abide any more of your outbursts!" She aimed her ruler at the door. "Go to the office this instant!"

Slowly, very slowly, I dragged myself out of my desk. It wasn't that I'd never been to the office before; I was just disappointed I hadn't gotten to use my hammer.

I didn't even glance at Robby's trophy or Daniel's prize-winning sketches on my way to the office. Robby was the only quarterback who'd led our team to a state championship, and Daniel's artwork was so good that they'd put it on display. Normally, I liked looking at these friendly reminders, but today, they just emphasized that Robby and Daniel were dead.

I'd barely trudged through the door when Gracie burst to

her feet. It took all my willpower not to turn right around. If I'd remembered that Monday was Gracie's day in the office, I might have made more of an effort to stay on Miss Fightmaster's good side.

"Where's Miss Shepherd?" I asked. She was the *real* secretary. Gracie was just a lowly student aide.

She waved my question away. "What happened this time, Ella Mae?"

"Nothing," I said. "Really. I just asked a question."

"You never just ask a question."

I shrugged. She had a point.

Gracie bit her lip. "So what happened?"

"Oh, Miss Fightmaster was just sayin' something silly about acorns, and I simply asked if they had DNA."

"What's DNA?" Gracie asked.

"Deoxyribo-something-or-other."

I expected Gracie to gasp or at least press me for details, but she only sat there smiling, like I had meat loaf for brains. So Auntie Mildred hadn't told them. Somehow, I wasn't surprised.

Gracie wasn't authorized to administer judgment, so we had to wait for Mr. Lloyd (who was holed up in his office, doing whatever principals did when they weren't tormenting their students). The sunburst clock struck noon before he finally came out, but since the lunch bell had just rung, he only took one look at me before he waved me out the door.

I dashed out of the office, eager to catch back up to Theo.

Since our mamas packed our lunches, we always headed to the playground as soon as the bell rang (and since I often got sent to the office, he was used to bringing mine).

"We spent the morning dissecting acorns," he said, swinging his lunch box exuberantly. "Walter smashed his to smithereens as soon as Miss Fightmaster turned her back, but I pried off my cupule—that's the little cap thing on top—without damaging the inside."

I tightened my grip on my lunch pail. "It figures." I'd asked for a lunch box the same as Theo's, but Mama had decided the lunch pail still worked fine.

"You can't let her bait you," he said as he pulled open the door. "If you just kept your mouth shut, she wouldn't know you exist."

"Is that your goal in life, to fade into the background?"

"Yes," Theo said. "At least as far as Miss Fightmaster's concerned."

I couldn't argue with that logic. I raised a hand to shield my eyes as I led the way across the blacktop. For once, the sun had burned off the clouds that drifted ashore every night, so the playground almost sparkled. It was a sight to see.

We didn't waste any words as we unpacked our lunches and made our usual trades: one of Mama's snickerdoodles for Auntie Mildred's store-bought pudding and a handful of green grapes for one or two Keebler crackers. Other folks might have liked having scores of fair-weather friends, but I just needed Theo, and he just needed me.

We were halfway through our lunches when a scuffle caught my eye (or, more precisely, the wall of shoulders that had formed around the scuffle).

"You see that?" I asked Theo, scrambling onto a tree stump.

"Of course I see it," Theo said. "It's twenty feet away."

I chucked a grape at his forehead. "That wasn't what I meant."

Theo polished off the last of his bologna sandwich. "If you were askin' if I wanted to leave the shelter of this shade tree and stick my nose in where it doesn't belong, then the answer is—"

I didn't wait for him to finish, just launched myself off the tree stump. I was still a few feet away when I heard Walter shout, "I said, get off!"

While the object of Walter's bullying fumbled for a reply, I pushed through the wall of shoulders. Walter had a fistful of the Dent boy's collar and was trying to drag him off the seesaw, but the boy refused to budge. He couldn't have been more than six, but he'd wrapped his arms around the handle and his legs around the seat.

"What's the matter, Walter?" I asked. "Can't handle that little kid?"

Walter didn't let go of the boy, but he did set him down as he scanned the nervous crowd. When his eyes settled on me, I stuck out my chin.

Walter instantly brightened. "Oh, look, it's the escapee from the funny farm!" He flung the boy to the side.

The boy hit the ground hard, though he managed to hang on to the seesaw. Once he dusted himself off, he stuck out his tongue, then carefully fixed his collar. I grinned despite myself. Walter might have had his back turned, but the boy was a warrior, no doubt about it.

"What's the food like?" Walter asked. "I hope they at least had Jell-O. You must have been in there for weeks!"

"We were only there for an hour. And it wasn't a funny farm, it was a lab."

"Ooh, a lab!" Walter said as he slithered closer. "Did they treat you like a rat, make you run through the mazes?"

"No," I replied without giving up ground. "They brought a man back to life."

"They brought a man back to *life*? Was it a zombie or something?"

While the crowd giggled like lamebrains, my hands clenched into fists. "I'm not makin' this up. I saw him with my own two eyes."

"Quiet, Ella Mae!" a familiar voice growled, though I was surprised to hear it here. I hadn't thought that Theo would leave the shelter of our shade tree. "He's just tryin' to get you to say things you'll regret."

It was awfully sporting of Theo to stick his nose in where it didn't belong, but I still pretended that I hadn't heard. Daddy might have brushed me off, and Mama might have shushed me, but now I had a chance to tell the whole world what I'd seen. They would have to believe me.

"They looked like grown-ups, but they weren't. They walked and talked like babies."

The crowd couldn't even hear. They were too busy laughing like a pack of wild hyenas.

I jumped onto the seesaw. "One of them was Japanese."

At least that shut them up. A shock wave rippled through the crowd, knocking everyone back. It was so far-fetched, so unbelievable, that it had to be true.

Walter jumped onto the seesaw, too. "If there's a Jap, I say we stone him!"

The crowd cheered, but I clenched my teeth. The thought of watching Walter do something to the Japanese man was enough to make me sick. It would be like watching Auntie Mildred get jabbed with that needle.

I locked my wrist, then lined it up with my elbow. Daddy had once spent a day teaching me how to punch, since he'd boxed back in college and hadn't wanted to see his expertise go to waste. It had been a few years since the lesson, but there were some things that you never forgot.

I didn't waste any movement, just went straight for his stomach. I was about to make contact when a pair of rough hands captured me from behind.

Mrs. Temple's plump face reminded me of a tomato. "Ella Mae, what were you thinking?"

I tried—and failed—to get away. "I was thinkin' my knuckles might not hurt so much if I hit him in the stomach."

"That wasn't what I meant," she said, sighing, as she

dragged me back inside. And that was how I wound up in the office for the second time in one day.

The sunburst clock ticked off the minutes while I waited for the bigwigs to determine my fate. They'd probably left me out here so I could think about my choices, but I wasn't thinking about my choices so much as imagining what it would have felt like to connect with Walter's solar plexus.

Finally, the inner door squeaked open, and Gracie reappeared (though she refused to meet my gaze). "I'm going to have to call your mama."

"Go ahead," I replied, nodding toward the telephone. Mama would straighten this out.

Not surprisingly, their conversation only lasted a second. No sooner had the words "Japanese man" left her lips than Gracie blinked and said good-bye.

I leaned forward. "What'd she say?"

"She's on her way," Gracie said as she hung up the receiver. "She wants to have a talk. In person."

I couldn't help but smile smugly.

8

Mama blew into the office like a Santa Ana wind, full of hot air and dusty heat. I settled in to watch the fireworks, but she didn't want to talk to Mr. Lloyd or even Gracie. She wanted to talk to *me*.

Gracie tried to talk her out of it, but Mama was insistent, so Gracie handed her the form to sign me out of school. When she got to the reason, Mama scribbled, "None of your beeswax," then chucked the pen at Gracie and took hold of my hand. I expected her to drag me home (and string me up by my toenails), but she took me to the drugstore, which doubled as St. Jude's soda fountain.

I glanced up at Mama. "Is this supposed to be my reward?" She knew how much I loved the world-famous Mother Lode, seven scoops of chocolate ice cream with all the fixings.

Mama shook her head. "Think of it more as a bribe."

If I'd been wary before, I was downright suspicious now. She had me so on edge that when the bell above the door jingled, I nearly dove for cover.

Chester Richmond, St. Jude's resident soda jerk, did his best not to notice. As the dispenser of sodas and keeper

57

of the bar, he'd learned how to ignore the strange things people did. "Well, if it isn't my favorite customer!" he said, flinging his dishrag over his shoulder.

I held up both hands. "Since you and me both know you're only usin' me to get to Gracie, let's just skip the small talk and cut straight to my ice cream."

Chester winked, actually winked, before he headed off to get my Mother Lode. I scrambled onto a bar stool to await his return, but Mama just sagged against the nearest counter. She looked like she was carrying the weight of the world on her shoulders (or at least the weight of St. Jude).

I knotted my arms across my chest. "I'm not sorry I creamed Walter."

"Gracie said you *didn't* cream him."

"It's the thought that counts."

Mama chuckled tiredly. "I'm actually more interested in your conversation with Miss Fightmaster."

I blushed despite myself. "I really wasn't tryin' to interrupt her lesson. I just wanted to know."

"I believe you," Mama said. "And it ain't wrong to ask questions. I just don't think St. Jude's ready for the answers we've been gettin'."

"Is that why you didn't tell Daddy?"

Mama sighed. "It's complicated."

Before I had a chance to press her, Chester came back with my Mother Lode. "That's seven scoops of chocolate ice cream with caramel sauce and slivered almonds." He set the bowl down with a flourish.

"And you even remembered not to douse it with whipped cream." I shoved a spoonful in my mouth. "I'll put in a good word for you with Gracie."

He winked again. "I'd like that."

"Want a bite?" I asked Mama.

Mama shook her head distractedly. She was too busy watching Chester, who'd pulled the dishrag off his shoulder and was wiping down the counter at the other end of the bar. When he turned his attention to the sink, where a heap of sudsy dishes was waiting to be rinsed, she finally relaxed.

"Let me ask you something," Mama said. "How'd you feel when Dr. Franks first showed us that pod?"

I shoved another spoonful in my mouth as I thought back on that day. The moment when the Japanese man stumbled out of that horse pill would be forever etched on my memory, but the details were already fading. I could barely remember what the place had smelled like, let alone how I'd felt.

"I don't know," I admitted. "I don't think I believed him."

"I didn't," Mama said. "Not even when it split in half and spit out that Japanese man. I was sure it was a trick designed to reopen old wounds—or maybe to get your auntie to give 'em more than Robby's blood."

I licked a glob of caramel off the spoon. "It sure looked like you believed him."

"Well, after I thought about it for a second, I realized it couldn't be a trick."

"Is that why you got angry?"

"I wasn't angry," Mama said. "I was afraid. More afraid, in fact, than I've ever been of anything."

The only other time I'd seen Mama scared was on the day we'd received the telegram:

```
PFC DANIEL HIGBEE WAS KILLED IN ACTION STOP
YOU MAY EXPECT HIS BODY IN THE NEXT THREE TO
FOUR WEEKS STOP SO SORRY FOR YOUR LOSS STOP
```

"Why were you afraid?" I asked. "Is it because of what he is?"

Mama's eyes widened. "I'm *terrified* of what he is."

That reminded me of the conclusion Auntie Mildred had come to about Robby's death, but before I had a chance to ask Mama what she meant, Chester turned off the water. Mama clammed up at once, but he didn't even glance in our direction, just dried his hands off on a towel and disappeared through a door marked EMPLOYEES ONLY.

Mama sighed again. "But I'm not afraid of him for the reasons you might think."

It was like she'd read my mind.

"He's not natural," she went on. "Dr. Franks took a flake of blood and turned it into a man—and not even the right man, but some other man entirely. That's God's work, Ella Mae." She pressed her lips into a line. "Or maybe it's not even that."

I'd thought the same thing, but hearing those words

come out of someone else's mouth made them seem more threatening. "What are you tryin' to say?"

"I'm sayin' the less Daddy knows, the better, to answer your first question."

I crinkled my nose. Daddy said she liked to talk until she finally made sense, but sometimes it took a while.

"Don't worry, sweetness," Mama said. "These things always have a way of workin' themselves out." She tugged one of my braids. "But in the meantime, maybe you should try to stay on Miss Fightmaster's good side. And steer clear of Walter. Heaven only knows we have enough numbskulls to deal with."

I couldn't agree more.

9

Mama was more than ready for the next observation. That Friday, she suggested that I go to bed early so I'd be ready to leave first thing Saturday morning. When I asked her why she was so anxious to get jabbed with a needle, she said some things were more important than keeping yourself safe. Dr. Franks might have won the battle, but he wasn't going to win the war.

But if that was the case, we were going to have to win it with one less ally. When we swung by Auntie Mildred's place on our way to the lab, Gracie was the one who actually answered the door. Mama yelled something about courage and taking a stand against evil, but Auntie Mildred ignored her, and Gracie had no choice but to bid her good day. I could tell she wanted to ask what the fuss was about, but she was too chicken to do it. It was probably just as well. I doubted I could have explained even if I'd wanted to.

We pulled into the parking lot of Ingolstadt Laboratories just a few minutes late. A convoy of black Cadillacs had parked next to the curb, but they were the only cars in sight.

"Where is everyone?" I asked as I climbed out of the Studebaker.

"Beats me," Mama said.

As we marched into the lobby, Mama squeezed my hand. I couldn't decide whether it was more for my benefit or hers.

"I'm Anna Higbee," she said. The secretary didn't look familiar, but then, they never did. "We have an appointment with Dr. Franks."

The secretary didn't bother to look up from her paperback. "Dr. Franks canceled his appointments. He doesn't like entertaining when Dr. Pauling's around."

"Who's Dr. Pauling?" I asked.

"The head honcho," she said, nodding toward the portrait. "Word on the street is that Dr. Franks hasn't been entirely up-front about the research he's been doing, but I wouldn't mind if they sacked him. The guy's a real drag. Did you know he tried to fire me when I forgot to spit out my gum?" She pretended to blow a bubble. "Like I said, a real drag."

"Don't worry," I said. "We're good at keepin' secrets."

"Well," Mama said after clearing her throat, "as much as we'd like to sit around here and chat, I'm afraid we have to go."

The secretary motioned toward the door at the far end of the lobby. "Well, then, go ahead."

"Just like that?" Mama asked.

"Just like that," she replied. "Unless you'd rather reschedule?"

"Oh, no, that won't be necessary." Mama dipped her head. "Thank you."

The secretary grinned. "Of course." And with that, she waved us through.

I wasn't sure exactly why the secretary hadn't sent us packing, but I wasn't about to question her. Thankfully, the other secretaries didn't bother us as we made our way into the lab. In fact, the last one even took us directly to Dr. Franks, who was pacing in a room like the one from our first visit. But no giant horse pill waited on the other side of the glass, just a dozen metal tables with pairs of plastic chairs.

Dr. Franks didn't turn around when the door opened behind him. "We need to do this quickly, Jackson, before Linus takes his tour."

"Who's Linus?" I replied.

Dr. Franks twisted around, clutching his clipboard like a shield. "I thought I told Imogene to cancel my appointments!"

"Guess we didn't get the memo," I said.

Before Dr. Franks could come up with a suitable reply, another door opened, and a team of assistants poured into the room, spreading out around the tables like ants around a picnic. They looked like the same assistants from the week before, though it was hard to say for sure. President Truman could have been hiding behind one of those masks, and I wouldn't have known.

I sidled up to Dr. Franks and sneaked a peek at his clipboard (a move I'd learned from Sergeant Friday). His arm was covering most of it, but I could make out the man's

64

picture—it was definitely him—and the first part of his name.

"It's Takuma!" I said.

Dr. Franks turned the clipboard upside down. "Hasn't anyone ever taught you to mind your own business?"

"But this *is* our business," Mama said as she arched an eyebrow.

Dr. Franks resisted, but he was no match for Mama's eyebrow. It only took a second for him to hand the clipboard over.

Mama's gaze darted from one end to the other. "He was born in mid-May, same as Daniel."

I tilted it down so I could get a better look. "And he died on Iwo Jima, same as Robby."

While me and Mama exchanged a loaded glance, Dr. Franks took back his clipboard. "Bring him in, Jackson," he said into the intercom.

The door opened again, and the Japanese man shuffled in. He wasn't wearing handcuffs, but he looked like a prisoner just the same. His head was bowed, his shoulders were hunched, and his black hair was matted with grease. I wished I'd brought a comb to give him.

"Where are the others?" Mama asked.

"The others?" Dr. Franks replied.

"Yes, the others!" Mama said. "Your band of half-formed misfits! What have you done with them?"

Dr. Franks stuck out his chin. "I haven't done anything. They're . . . unavailable."

"Unavailable as in they've been detained or as in they've left the building?"

Dr. Franks glowered. "Now, that is *certainly* none of your business."

Unaware of the drama unfolding on our side of the glass, the Japanese man took a seat at a nearby table. He hunkered down instinctively, as if he'd gotten used to cowering, but when he spotted me, he sat back up. I wanted to press my hand to the window, see if he'd press his back, but he wouldn't have been able to reach.

Dr. Franks glanced at his clipboard. "He's made remarkable improvement over the last several days. Physically, he was already operating in the ninety-sixth percentile, and I'm happy to report that his brain is catching up."

"How do you know?" I replied.

"Because we've been monitoring his brain activity." Dr. Franks checked both ways. "And because he *talks*."

Mama's eyes narrowed. "What's he said?"

"Oh, nothing of substance. 'I'm tired.' 'I want an apple.' 'I need to urinate.' It's in Japanese, regrettably, which is why we've brought in a translator, but it supports our working theory that he *is* Takuma Sato. That I've literally brought a man back from the grave."

I scrunched up my nose. "Didn't you already think that?"

"Well, there was always the concern that we created a facsimile—a lookalike, if you will." Dr. Franks licked his lips. "But it looks like I've regenerated Takuma Sato himself."

I shrank away from Dr. Franks, who was eyeing the

Japanese man like a starving man might eye a piece of prime rib.

"Let's get started, Jackson," he said into the nearby intercom. Over his shoulder, he added, "And since you're already here, you might as well stay to observe."

"Oh, don't you worry," Mama said, thumping him on the back. "We won't be goin' anywhere."

One of the assistants, likely Jackson, sat down at the same table. "Please state your name for the record."

Another assistant leaned over the Japanese man's shoulder and mumbled something in his ear.

"Takuma Sato," the man said.

The other assistants scribbled down his answer, though they must have known what he was going to say.

"And your date of birth?" Jackson asked.

The translator mumbled something in his ear again, and the man replied in Japanese.

The translator cleared her throat. "He doesn't understand the question, sir." Her voice was high and squeaky.

Jackson leaned forward. "Then ask him when he was born."

The translator asked, and the Japanese man answered.

"He's lost track of the days," the translator said slowly, "but he thinks it's been fifteen since he woke up in the sub." Her eyes crinkled at the corners, and I got the impression she was smiling. "Probably not the answer you were looking for."

Dr. Franks's face turned purple. "Don't write that down!" he barked.

The assistants' hands froze over their clipboards. A few tried to erase whatever they'd just written (but only when they thought he wasn't looking).

"And Miss Ryland," Dr. Franks went on, "please refrain from sermonizing on the subject's answers!"

Miss Ryland ducked her head, though her eyes didn't stop smiling. I pressed a hand over my mouth to cover my own grin.

Jackson removed his mask, revealing a stubbly chin. "We're not communicating very well, are we?" He propped his elbows on his knees and looked the Japanese man in the eyes. "We just want to figure out if you remember where you came from."

Miss Ryland whispered something to the man, who slowly shook his head.

"I don't see why you care," I said after Dr. Franks chucked his own clipboard, "seeing as you already know."

Self-consciously, he retrieved his clipboard. "But I want to know if *he* knows."

"One out of two ain't all that bad."

Dr. Franks harrumphed.

"Well, maybe he'll remember soon." Under my breath, I added, "He *has* been dead, you know."

Dr. Franks rolled his eyes. "I know."

The interview continued without another interruption. Jackson asked the Japanese man every question he could think of, including what six times thirty-nine was (two hundred and thirty-four) and what the Japanese man liked to do (talk to Jackson, mostly, but also eat fruit cocktail). I thought his answers were impressive—I wouldn't have remembered my times tables if I'd been dead for seven years—but Dr. Franks just stood there scowling.

Finally, Jackson asked, "Do you remember how you died?"

A haunting silence filled the room. I gripped the windowsill instinctively. He hadn't remembered much, just a vague flash or two, but he might remember this. If you cut out the years between his death and rebirth, it had only happened a few weeks ago. And if he remembered how he'd died, would he remember killing Robby?

The Japanese man looked around, then set his sights on me. I couldn't look away.

Last summer, me and Theo had found a stray dog at the pier. Theo had scampered off, blubbering something about rabies—if those Clausens knew anything, it was how to retreat—but I'd held my ground. It was like me and that dog had been able to say a bunch of things without saying one word. Eventually, Theo had come back and convinced me not to leash him, but a part of me had always wondered what friends we might have been if I'd been brave enough to take that dog home. As I locked eyes with the Japanese man, I wondered the same thing.

The man dropped his gaze first and whispered something to Miss Ryland.

"He doesn't remember," she murmured, keeping her eyes on the table.

Dr. Franks pounced on the intercom. "He must remember

something," he hissed. "So push him, Jackson. Make him work. We need precise responses if we want to be able to complete a full analysis." Under his breath, he added, "You *know* he's our last hope."

This seemed like just the sort of thing that Sergeant Friday would write down in his little black notepad. But I didn't have a black notepad (or a way to carry it, for that matter), so I committed it to memory.

Jackson shifted uncomfortably. "Is there anything you'd like to add?"

Miss Ryland posed the question, then waited for his response. The man drew a quick breath, then distinctly said, "No."

He said it in Japanese, but somehow, I understood (and for some reason, I believed).

Dr. Franks smacked the intercom. "He's lying!" he insisted, then spun sharply around and leveled a finger at Mama. "This is your fault, isn't it? *You* planted that sample. *You* sabotaged my research. You're probably in league with the boys from Cavendish themselves! But how could they have known my other subjects wouldn't—?"

Dr. Franks stopped himself before he spilled the beans, but the damage was already done. He'd all but admitted that *something* was happening. Unfortunately, Mama was less interested in pumping him for details than setting the record straight.

"No one sent us," she said as calmly as a spring morning.

But Dr. Franks was just getting warmed up. While the

assistants' jaws slowly dropped, he whined about everything from English food (which apparently tasted like shoes) to the boys from Cavendish (whose names were James and Francis).

The Japanese man, on the other hand, watched me through the glass. Neither of us said a word, but we still had a conversation. He asked about our house and whether the trees in our backyard were big enough to climb, but it seemed like he was really asking if I was going to take him home.

10

I tapped Dr. Franks's shoulder. "When do we get to take him home?"

"Excuse me?" he asked.

I cleared my throat. "I said, when do we get to take him home?" I said it carefully so he wouldn't misunderstand. "That is what you've been tryin' to get us to do from day one."

"Well, yes," he said, retreating. "But I thought—I just assumed—"

"We wouldn't want him?" Mama asked.

"Well, yes!" Dr. Franks shouted as he fiddled with his sleeve. "In case you haven't noticed, he's a Jap."

"Oh, we've noticed," I said.

"Then you also must have noticed that he doesn't belong to you. What makes you think you have the right to steal ten years' worth of research?"

I threw up my arms. "I thought you wanted us to take him!"

"I did," he said. "Before . . ."

"Before *what*?" Mama pressed.

I bit my lip to keep from squealing. Mama had finally asked the all-important question. Dr. Franks was finally going to have to tell us the truth.

He opened his mouth to answer, and for a second, I really thought he was going to say it. But then he snapped his mouth shut. "Before I changed my mind."

I stuck both hands on my hips. If he wanted to play that game, then I'd play it, too. "Well, I'm not changin' mine."

"Then it appears we're at an impasse."

"What's an impasse?" I asked.

"A stalemate," Mama said. "Which means we'll need someone to break it."

Dr. Franks harrumphed. "Well, it shouldn't be *you*."

"No," Mama agreed, "it should be someone impartial, someone—"

"In charge?" I asked.

"Exactly," Mama said.

I smiled mysteriously. "Then I know just the person."

Mama cocked an eyebrow, and a part of me worried that she was going to try to stop me. But instead of getting in my way, she got out of it. And smiled. *Go ahead, sweetness,* that smile seemed to say. *If anyone can do this, you can.*

As it turned out, the head honcho was pretty easy to find. I just shouted Dr. Pauling's name as I dashed up and down the halls, taking random lefts and rights. Every intersection looked the same, so it wasn't hard to choose. Doors slid open in my wake, ejecting scads of assistants, who trailed along behind me like a ticker-tape parade, lab coats and clipboards fluttering. Luckily, they weren't as good at playing tag as I was.

The men in black suits, on the other hand, were another matter altogether.

I slammed into the first after taking a wrong turn. He tried to grab me while I blinked the stars out of my eyes, but I recovered just in time to duck under his arms. Regrettably, the second was harder to elude. He seized me from behind while I was distracted by the first, then picked me up as easily as if I were a string bean. I liked to think I'd eaten more Mother Lodes than that.

The cavalry showed up after the man tossed me over his shoulder. At least the assistants looked like they could barely breathe.

I stuck out my chin. "I want to talk to Dr. Pauling."

One of the assistants sneered. "He isn't here, silly girl."

But I wasn't discouraged. "I have reason to think he is."

At least that shut him up. He backed off just in time for Dr. Franks to turn the corner. Mama was hot on his heels.

"You will put her down this instant," Mama hissed after sizing up the situation, "or I will gut you where you stand."

Dr. Franks elbowed around her. "You will do no such thing. That child is a menace to society, and I insist that you restrain her."

The man glanced at Mama, then Dr. Franks, then Mama again, then put me down. He must have been more afraid of Mama (and I couldn't say I blamed him).

Dr. Franks bristled. "If you won't detain her, then I demand that you expel them."

The man checked with his partner, then mumbled, "Sorry, doc. I can't kick anyone out without Dr. Pauling's say-so."

Dr. Franks's cheeks paled. For a second, maybe less, I actually felt sorry for him.

"Come with me," the man said.

Me and Mama scurried after him, afraid of getting lost. Dr. Franks delayed for as long as he could, then, grudgingly, clomped after us. If he wanted Dr. Pauling to hear his side of the story, he had no choice but to follow.

The man led us through the labyrinth like a bloodhound on the scent. He never paused to get his bearings or even check his nose. His partner hemmed us in, probably to keep us from exploring.

Eventually, we arrived at an unfamiliar elevator. It smelled like pencil shavings, which reminded me of Daniel. He'd once drawn a dragon for me on the back of an old napkin, with two ketchup spots for eyes. The napkin was still tucked inside my sock drawer (along with my favorite seashell and a two-dollar bill that Grandpa Willy had passed down to me).

No one dared to speak as the elevator rattled upward. When the door opened again, I raised a hand to shield my eyes, since this floor was much brighter than the ones below it. Maybe Mother Nature had come up here to hide.

The man knocked on a door, then turned the shiny knob,

revealing a small lobby with an even smaller desk. The room wasn't as fancy—after all, the doors had *knobs*—but the tulips made it friendlier. It only had one other door, which was firmly shut.

The secretary eyed us intently as the man explained the situation, but instead of pumping us for details, she invited us to sit. I was the only one who did, though I couldn't have said why. I thought the chairs looked comfy, and there really was no telling how long we'd have to wait.

But I'd barely gotten settled when another man opened the second door. "What is it?" he demanded. His suit was brown, not black, but he looked too young to be the man from the portrait.

"Three visitors for Dr. Pauling," the secretary said.

"Dr. Pauling isn't taking visitors."

"He'll want to take these ones."

The man sighed. "Very well. But if this is another singing telegram, we might just have to fire you."

I took that as my cue to barge into the room, which turned out to be a disappointment. I'd expected a smart office, with floor-to-ceiling bookcases and maybe a telescope, but except for a few men and a funny-looking model, it was perfectly empty.

"Dr. Pauling?" I asked.

One of the men looked up from the model. "Yes?" His nose was big and bulbous, and little tufts of hair were sprouting from his ears.

I folded my arms across my chest. "You have my cousin, and we want him back."

"Your cousin?" Dr. Pauling asked.

I felt my cheeks redden. "Well, that was who he was supposed to be."

Mama cleared her throat. "What my daughter means is that there's a boy downstairs whose well-being we feel liable for."

I didn't know what "liable" meant, but Dr. Pauling clearly did, because he straightened up.

"He's been involved in an experiment," Mama went on. "But the experiment's over now, and Dr. Franks won't let him go."

Dr. Pauling raised his eyebrows. "Victor, care to explain?"

Dr. Franks waved that off. "They're obviously exaggerating," he said, but even though he sounded sure, his almost-trembling knees betrayed him.

Dr. Pauling rubbed his jaw, then motioned us into the room. "Close the door," he said, and the man in the brown suit closed it.

We arranged ourselves into a crooked line, with Dr. Franks on my left side and Mama on my right. The men looked us up and down, some with interest, some with the same unconcealed contempt Miss Fightmaster reserved for troublemakers and Charles Darwin. Still, I didn't look away. If I looked away, they might decide I wasn't serious, and I was as serious as sin.

"Now," Dr. Pauling said, making himself comfortable (or as comfortable as you could make yourself in a room without a chair), "I'd like to hear this story one small detail at a time."

Dr. Franks chuckled uneasily. "It is rather amusing."

"I'm sure it is," he said. "But I'd like to hear it from the girl."

I resisted the urge to stick my tongue out. "Well, the whole thing started with Robby."

"Who's Robby?" Dr. Pauling asked.

"My cousin," I replied. "Except the experiment didn't go like Dr. Franks thought it would."

"Do they ever?" he asked, smiling.

The other men snickered, except for Dr. Franks. He rocked back and forth like he had to use the bathroom.

"Anyway," I said, "we have this Japanese man now, but Dr. Franks decided that we can't take him home."

Dr. Pauling rubbed his eyes. "A Japanese man? Where'd *he* come from?"

"Forgive the intrusion," Dr. Franks cut in, "but I don't think this line of questioning is strictly necessary—"

"Victor," Dr. Pauling said, "as I already told you, I want to hear this from the girl." He returned his attention to me. "So where did he come from, this Japanese man?"

"I don't know," I said. "Japan?"

The other men snickered again, like I'd said something funny. Scientists were peculiar folks.

"Excuse me," Mama said, "but we just want to know if he can hold the boy indefinitely."

"Of course not," Dr. Pauling said. "The Institute's not in the habit of incarcerating volunteers." He arched an eyebrow at me. "But how do you know this Japanese man wants to go home with you?"

I thought back on those times when we locked eyes through the window. "I don't know," I admitted. "But I know *I* want to take him, and it seems like that should count."

This time, no one snickered. Dr. Pauling rubbed his jaw again and studied the model. At first, it had reminded me of a spiral staircase, but the more I stared at it, the more I decided that it looked like an exotic flower.

Finally, he glanced at Mama. "You support this rescue mission?"

Mama nodded. "Absolutely."

Then he glanced at Dr. Franks. "And they signed the standard contract?"

Dr. Franks harrumphed. "Well, Mrs. Clausen did."

"Who's Mrs. Clausen?" Dr. Pauling asked, then swiftly shook his head. "Oh, never mind. Don't tell me. I probably don't want to know."

I snorted. "You're not kiddin'."

Dr. Pauling mopped his forehead with an off-white handkerchief. "It sounds like we have no choice."

Dr. Franks nearly leaped out of his lab coat. "Well, of

course we have a choice! We can't concede the race to James and Francis!"

"We're not conceding *anything*." Dr. Pauling gripped his shoulder. "Certainly your line of research isn't dependent on one subject."

Dr. Franks started to answer, then changed his mind at the last second.

"You see? Things will work out." Dr. Pauling glanced at me. "Was there anything else?"

I shook my head. "We're good."

He held out his hand. "It's been a pleasure doing business."

I grinned as I said, "Likewise."

11

We picked up the Japanese man back on the first floor. Thankfully, someone had managed to find him a pair of pants and a clean shirt. I could have handled riding home next to a Japanese man or a man in his pajamas, but certainly not both.

I stared at the man, and he stared back at me. He smelled like Dr. Franks's sickly sweet cologne, but it didn't seem fair to hold that against him. Maybe it wasn't his cologne but the building itself.

I jerked a thumb over my shoulder. "You're comin' with us."

The Japanese man blinked.

"Do you understand?" I motioned back and forth between us. "We're breakin' you out!"

"You're wasting your breath, foolish girl," Dr. Franks said, sniffing. "He doesn't speak English."

"Neither do Uncle George's sheep," I said, "but I still talk to them."

Dr. Franks's lip curled, but instead of answering, he stalked away.

I waited until he disappeared, then asked the Japanese man, "Are you ready?"

The man bowed. "Are-ee-got-toe."

I decided that meant yes.

Mama took the long way home, winding aimlessly past orange groves before merging onto Highway 1. The beach looked especially inviting after our long day at the lab, but Mama said we couldn't stop, since Daddy was going to have enough questions as it was.

Daddy was a Northerner, with a family tree that stretched all the way back to Plymouth Rock, so he hadn't had a problem when the Dodgers hired Jackie Robinson or when Mr. Dent married his Hawaiian bride. But then, Jackie Robinson and Mrs. Dent had never tried to sink our navy, then invited themselves to our house.

"What's this?" Daddy asked as soon as we walked through the door.

"He's not a what, Daddy, he's a who."

"His name is Takuma," Mama said as she tugged off her hat.

"Takuma?" Daddy asked, spitting that word out of his mouth like a hunk of rotten meat.

Mama sighed. "It's complicated."

Daddy looked back and forth between us, then raked a hand through his dark hair. "Ella Mae, your mother and I need to have a little chat."

This was code for *Me and Mama are about to have a fight,*

so if you don't want to get your eyebrows singed, you'd better scuttle off.

"Come on," I told the man. "I'll show you around."

Daddy's glower made it clear that he didn't approve, but what else were we supposed to do, hide in the bomb shelter out back? I led the man into the kitchen (since the first thing every guest should know was where Mama hid the snickerdoodles), but when I realized that I could hear what Mama and Daddy were saying, I just stood there listening.

"Where in heaven's name did you find a Jap?" he asked.

"You wouldn't believe me if I told you."

"Well, then, would I believe why you chose to bring him *here*?"

"He needed a place to stay," she said. "If you'd only seen where he was livin' . . ."

"It's one thing to be charitable, but it's another to be mad. What are we supposed to *do* with him?"

"I don't know," she admitted.

I backed away from the archway. I'd never heard Mama sound so unsure before. What if we'd made the wrong choice? It was too late to take it back.

"Come on," I mumbled tiredly. The snickerdoodles would have to wait. I didn't want to hear what Mama and Daddy were saying anymore.

I led the man upstairs, since it seemed like the safest place. The old stairs creaked beneath my feet but not beneath the man's. His shoes must have been quieter.

At the top of the stairs, I reached for the door to Daniel's room, then dropped my hand at the last second. It seemed wrong to barge in unannounced. But then, Daniel hadn't minded when he was alive, so maybe he wouldn't mind now. I drew a bracing breath, then slowly turned the knob.

A rush of stale air greeted us, though it wasn't as stale as it might have been. Mama aired the room out every Monday while she vacuumed and dusted, though it was more of a habit than a necessity. Mama said the dead made fewer messes than the living.

I'd always believed that. Now I wasn't so sure.

"My brother's room," I said as I waved the man inside.

His eyes widened to the size of chocolate coins as he stepped across the threshold.

I tried to see what he was seeing, and it wasn't hard. The furniture was nothing special, but the sketches were overwhelming. They covered every surface, including the walls, the desk, the dresser. Mama had framed them over time, so the room looked more like an art gallery than a place to sleep.

Daniel left for basic training a month before my fifth birthday, so I'd gotten to know him through his drawings. My favorite was the beachscape on the wall between our rooms. One day, I'd come downstairs to find him packing his knapsack. I'd asked where he was going, and when he said the beach, I'd begged to go along. We'd spent the afternoon building sand igloos—they were more interesting than castles—and playing hide-and-seek in the forest of logs under the pier. And drawing, of course. The tiny figure in the distance, the one with her arms spread out to the sky, was a four-year-old me.

"Daniel liked to draw," I said in case it wasn't obvious. "Folks around here said he was gonna be the next Norman Rockwell, but Daniel said he wasn't gonna be the next anyone. He was gonna be his own artist, and besides, Norman Rockwell was a painter."

The man spotted the beachscape and studied it intently.

"Do you like it?" I asked.

The man tilted his head as if deep in thought, then, finally, nodded.

"I like it, too," I said, smiling.

He smiled in return. It was probably instinctive, but I wanted to believe that he'd crawled inside my head and relived that day on the beach, that I'd shared a piece of Daniel with someone who hadn't known him before.

"I don't think we've been introduced," I said as I stuck out my hand. "My name is Ella Mae."

Instead of shaking it, he stared.

"You shake it," I explained, grabbing his right hand with my left and sticking it in mine.

The man didn't shake back.

"Never mind," I said as I let go of his hand and touched my chest instead. "My name is Ella Mae."

The man didn't react.

"Ella Mae," I said, pointing at myself. Then I pointed at him. "Takuma."

Something flashed in his dark eyes. It was a start, at least.

I touched his chest. "Takuma." Then I touched mine. "Ella Mae."

"Takuma," he finally said, pointing at himself. Then he pointed at me. "Ella Mae."

I grinned. "Sounds like you've got it."

Mama came upstairs after she and Daddy finished fighting and informed us that Takuma would spend the night in Daniel's room. We didn't have another bed, and making a grown man sleep on the floor was plum foolish (in her opinion). Also, the only floor was in the study, and Daddy didn't want Takuma messing up his things.

We went to bed early, but I couldn't fall asleep. For the first time in a long time, a real, live human being was in the room across the wall, and if I closed my eyes and let my memory go fuzzy, I could almost pretend that it was Daniel.

12

It felt like I'd just closed my eyes when Mama started clanking pots and pans bright and early the next morning. I jolted awake—she was fond of rousing me with cookware—but she was nowhere to be seen. I stuffed my head under my pillow and tried to fall asleep, but pillows weren't impervious to the smell of sizzling bacon. I stumbled down to breakfast without bothering to change.

"Why are you still wearin' your pajamas?" Mama asked. "You're gonna make us late for Sunday school!"

"I don't think I can go," I said, yawning enormously.

"You can yawn until the cows come home, but you're not skippin' church. You think Jesus took a Sunday off after fastin' forty days and nights?"

"I know it might surprise you, but I'm not as virtuous as Jesus."

"Which means you need to go to Sunday school even more than He did."

Daddy tromped into the kitchen. "Who's not going to Sunday school?" he asked as he finished knotting his tie.

"No one," Mama said, pointing her spatula at me. "Ella Mae's goin' to church whether she wants to or not."

"But I'm exhausted," I replied, plopping my chin into my hands.

Daddy nudged me with his elbow. "Had a wild night, did you?"

"Actually," I said, "I just couldn't fall asleep. It was weird to think that someone else was actually sleeping in the room right next to mine."

He didn't have a chance to answer before Takuma crept into the kitchen. His shirt from yesterday was rumpled, but he had comb tracks in his hair. Had he remembered how to do that, or had one of the assistants taught him?

Daddy unknotted his tie. "On second thought," he said as he retreated to the stairs, "I don't think this tie matches my suit."

"But your bacon!" I called after him. "It's gonna taste like rubber!"

"Quiet, sweetness," Mama said. "You need to let him go."

I wasn't so sure. Matching ties were one thing, but rubbery bacon was another.

Mama tipped her head toward Daddy's chair. "Have a seat, Takuma."

He hesitated for a moment, then, cautiously, sat down.

Mama dished him up a plate. "Here," she said, holding it out to him. "The best bacon and eggs you'll ever eat."

Takuma took it gingerly and set it on the table, but then

he just sat there staring. The eggs had already stopped steaming, and the bacon probably wasn't far behind.

"Didn't those cockamamie scientists teach you anything?" I asked as I reached across the table, seized a strip of bacon, and shoved it in his mouth.

Mama slapped my hand away. "Thank you for that demonstration, but he can manage on his own."

As if to prove her point, he retrieved the strip of bacon and took a dainty bite. I was watching it roll down his throat when Daddy reappeared. Takuma jumped out of his seat, but it was already too late.

Red-hot anger crawled up Daddy's neck, threatening to choke him, but he managed not to lose control. "What will he want next, the shirt right off my back?"

"Well, not that shirt," Mama said. "It has a grease stain on the collar. But it would be nice if he could borrow something from your closet."

Daddy's face flushed scarlet, but Mama pretended not to notice. Takuma sank back against the fridge and kept his eyes on the linoleum. I wanted to reach out, to touch him, but Daddy loomed between us, his eyes glowing like live coals.

Mama checked her Kit-Cat clock. The shifting eyes and ticktock tail had always struck me as funny, but for some reason, they seemed more sinister that morning. "Oh, I lost track of the time!" She snapped me with her apron. "Go and get dressed, Ella Mae."

"But I've only had one piece of bacon!"

"Not my fault," she said as she hurried toward the stairs. "Jed, we're gonna need that shirt!"

Daddy brought his fist down on the counter. "*No.*"

At least that got her attention. "Why not?" Mama asked.

"Because he's a Jap, for heaven's sake! You can't just stick him in a suit and pretend that he belongs!"

I grimaced for Takuma, who was now hunched over on the floor, hands wrapped around his knees to keep himself from tipping over. A shudder rippled through his shoulders every time he drew a breath, and I wished that I were brave enough to wrap my arms around his back.

I cleared my throat. "He could stay here." It wasn't a hug, but it was something.

"No, he couldn't," Daddy said. "I refuse to leave my home in the hands of an enemy."

"He's not an enemy," I said. "He can't even stand up straight."

Daddy's eyes narrowed. "It's probably an act."

"Then it's not a very good one."

Daddy frowned.

"If he can't stay here by himself, then I'll stay with him," I went on, trying to look suitably upset. "It'll be a shame to miss the lesson, but that's a price I'm willing to pay."

"You think I'd trust him with my daughter any more than I'd trust him with my home?" Daddy folded his arms across his chest. "If anyone stays, it will be me."

90

"Fat chance," Mama replied. "The last thing I want to do is bail you out of jail."

"We could all stay home," I said.

Mama dismissed this just as quickly. "Reverend Simms will wonder where we are."

"But we can't make him go," I peeped. "I mean, just look at him."

Mama looked at him, then sighed. "I guess you have a point." She chucked her apron on the counter. "But I expect these dishes to be done by the time that I get back!"

Mama grabbed her hat, then slammed the door shut on her heels. The spice rack didn't stop rattling until the Studebaker roared to life.

"I'll be in my study," Daddy said. "Holler if you need me."

"But what about the dishes?" I replied.

Daddy smiled fiercely. "I'm sure our *guest* won't mind earning his keep."

He retreated to his study before I had a chance to argue, but that was just as well. I'd never seen Daddy tell another man to do the dishes.

I waited until Daddy disappeared, then tiptoed toward Takuma. "It's all right," I said, imitating Gracie's soothing voice.

He looked up at me and blinked, so the imitation must have worked.

I held out my hand. "I promise I'm not gonna hurt you."

Gingerly, Takuma took it. I expected him to use it to haul

himself back up, but he just shook it, let it go, and stood up on his own.

I motioned toward the sink. "Have you ever done the dishes?"

He just stood there blinking.

"It figures," I grumbled as I drained the sink, then refilled it with hot water and another squirt of dish soap. Auntie Mildred would have praised me for being so sanitary, but I just didn't want to plunge my hands into scuzzy, lukewarm water.

I pointed at the table. "You think you can grab those plates?"

He must have understood the pointing. While I dug the rubber gloves out of the wash bin, he arranged the plates into a tower, breakfast dishes on the bottom, cups and silverware on top.

"You're pretty good at that," I said. "Were you a juggler in a circus?"

Instead of answering, he shrugged.

"Dr. Franks says you don't talk because you don't understand English, but I think you don't talk because he's a—"

"Me-zoo," he interrupted.

I blinked, then shook my head. "No, I was gonna say that I think Dr. Franks's a—"

"Me-zoo!"

I didn't have a chance to figure out what "me-zoo" meant before something sloshed against my wrists. I turned back toward the sink just as a sheet of sudsy water suddenly spilled over the edge, completely soaking my pajamas. The shock knocked me off balance, but Takuma grabbed my wrist to keep me from falling down. He hit the faucet with his free hand, and as we surveyed the damage, I finally figured out what he'd been trying to tell me: "me-zoo" had to mean water.

I met Takuma's eyes, which were as wide as dinner plates. Unfortunately, Daddy picked that moment to reappear in the archway.

"What's this?" he demanded.

Takuma dropped my hand.

Daddy clenched his teeth. "Did he hurt you, Ella Mae?"

"Of course not," I replied as I wrung out my sleeve. "Matter of fact, I think he saved me."

Daddy's gaze followed the drops that were raining from my sleeve, then darted back up to the sink. He might have missed the puddle, but it would have been hard to miss the suds.

"Clean this up," he said. "Ella Mae, go and get dressed."

"But I was the one who spilled—"

"I said, go and get dressed." His voice was flat and hard. "I think we've borne enough of your impertinence for now."

I opened my mouth to answer, then snapped it shut again. Daddy could only take so much impertinence (or so he'd told me before), and from the way his jaw was working, I could tell he was about to flip his lid. After sneaking one last peek at Takuma, I headed toward the stairs.

"Towels are in the cupboard," Daddy said to no one in

particular. He must have been talking to Takuma, but he refused to look at him. "I expect this kitchen to be as dry as the Mojave when I come back."

Takuma nodded stiffly. Daddy's instructions must have sounded like gibberish to his ears, but he didn't make excuses, just swept the dishrag off the counter and got down on his hands and knees. Water soaked into his pants, but he didn't seem to notice. Unfortunately, his pants were making more progress than the dishrag.

Daddy must have thought so, too, because he shouted, "In the cupboard!" When Takuma just kept mopping, he raked a hand through his dark hair. "Of all the Japs in all the towns in all the world, we get stuck with the idiot."

"He's not an idiot!" I said.

"I guess we'll see about that."

I caught a whiff of licorice as Daddy swept out of the kitchen, but instead of making me feel better, the familiar smell made me feel worse. If he hadn't smelled like licorice, I could have convinced myself it wasn't Daddy. But it *was* Daddy, and I knew him almost as well as I knew myself. If I tried to stay and help, he'd only make Takuma's life harder.

But there was one thing I could do. When I passed the cupboard with the towels, I flicked it open with my toe. And when Daddy came back later, the kitchen was as dry as the Mojave.

13

Takuma's daring rescue and subsequent cleanup went a long way toward convincing me that he was no idiot. While he dried off his hands, I assembled my visual aids: a slice of bread, a plastic cup, and the last roll of toilet paper. As I organized my treasures on Mama's Oriental rug (which probably wasn't Oriental, since Takuma had never noticed), he got comfy on the couch.

"Daddy thinks you're slow, but I think you just need some teachin', and you're probably a fast learner." I narrowed my eyes. "You *are* a fast learner, aren't you?"

Takuma nodded, sort of. Dr. Franks must have conditioned him.

"All right," I said, cracking my knuckles, "the first thing we've got to do is develop your vocabulary. You'll learn new words every day, but these are the important ones—food, water, and toilet paper." I pointed at each object in turn. "Or if you really have to go, you could just say, 'I have to pee.'"

He leaned forward, forehead crinkling, and picked up the slice of bread. "Food?" he said uncertainly as it crumbled in his hands.

"Yes!" I said. "Well, actually, it's a slice of bread, but you *can* eat it. Watch."

I grabbed the slice of bread and took an enormous bite. The bread was older than I'd thought it was, so it tasted slightly moldy and had the consistency of sawdust. I tried to swallow without chewing, but that only made things worse, since the bite of bread got stuck about halfway down my throat. While I thumped on my chest, Takuma's Adam's apple bobbed like he was trying to swallow for me.

"Well," I half said, half choked, "that's not usually so difficult."

Takuma didn't answer, just stared at me with worried eyes.

I stuck out my tongue to prove that I'd swallowed the bite, and he relaxed a little. I set the bread behind me, out of sight, and grabbed the plastic cup. Just because I'd nearly died didn't mean that every teaching moment would be life-or-death. If Miss Fightmaster could do it, then so could I.

"Water," I said, then shook my head. "Well, actually, it's a cup, but you put water in it." I pretended to turn a faucet on, then pretended to take a drink. "You drink water from the cup."

He took the cup. "Water." Then he pressed it to his lips. "Cup."

I sighed. "No, that ain't it."

Meekly, he returned the cup.

I was turning it over in my hands, trying to see it from another angle, when, suddenly, I did. "Me-zoo!"

Takuma's eyes lit up.

I pretended to turn a faucet on. "You put the me-zoo in the cup." Then I pretended to take a sip. "Then you drink the me-zoo."

Takuma grabbed it. "Cup." Then he tipped it over. "Water."

I leaped to my feet. "THAT'S IT!"

Takuma beamed, and I beamed back. I'd never thought much about Miss Fightmaster when I wasn't in school, but if this was how she felt after every successful lesson, then I could understand why she kept teaching them (and why her nostrils shriveled into slits every time I interrupted).

I was reaching for the roll of toilet paper when someone kicked the side door open. It was probably just Mama. I expected her to hang her hat on the coatrack in the entryway, but she only shuffled around the kitchen, rattling cookware as she went.

Me and Takuma exchanged a worried glance, then hurried into the kitchen, where Mama was rearranging pots and pans, moving them to one cupboard, then moving them right back.

"The kitchen looks nice," she said without meeting our eyes.

Guilt coated my tongue like a spoonful of cod liver oil. "I spilled the dishwater," I said, then jerked a thumb over my shoulder. "Takuma cleaned it up."

"Thank you," Mama said, though it didn't sound like she meant it.

Instead of answering, Takuma bowed.

At least that got her attention. Her eyes narrowed disapprovingly as they zeroed in on his ragged collar (which was still slightly damp). "Has it always looked like that?"

I threw up my arms. "Who cares what his collar looks like? I just taught him three whole words!"

"Is that all?" Mama asked, moving the dish soap to the pantry, then sticking it back under the sink.

I frowned. Daddy sometimes brushed me off (usually when he was reading the *Times*), but Mama always celebrated my accomplishments with me.

"Are you all right?" I asked. "Auntie Mildred didn't say something untoward, did she?"

"Auntie Mildred *always* says something untoward," she said. "But today's tirade was especially bad."

I crinkled my nose. "Did she say something about Takuma?"

"Not specifically," she said. "She'd never wave our dirty laundry under other people's noses. But she did make Sunday school awfully uncomfortable."

My hands balled into fists. "That ungrateful crone. Auntie Mildred was the one who started this!"

The words escaped my mouth before I could call them back, but apparently, Mama didn't mind that I'd called her sister a witch.

"Maybe," Mama mumbled. "But I've found it's always better to be a part of the solution."

• • •

At school the next day, I avoided Theo. I wasn't embarrassed about missing church so much as I was tired of coming up with good excuses. Fibbing was one thing, but fibbing convincingly was another, so I hid out in the cafeteria during lunch and ignored his whispers during class. As soon as the bell rang, I took off like a bottle rocket.

But Theo was ready for me. By the time I burst into the warm spring sun, he'd practically caught up.

"Ella Mae!" he said, letting the door clank shut behind him. That door had always made me think of prison cells and cold, dark places, but now I realized how little I really knew about being trapped. "Ella Mae, wait up!"

Though I didn't slow down, I did glance over my shoulder, and that was all it took for me to trip over a tree root. The old walnut tree had had it out for me since I'd broken off a lower branch at Halloween last year—I'd been Sacajawea; Theo had been Davy Crockett—and now it had finally gotten its revenge. In the time it took me to get back up, Theo had closed the gap between us and seized a handful of my book bag.

"What's goin' on?" he asked, bending down to catch his breath. "You're runnin' like you think Walter Lloyd is on your tail."

I tossed my braids over my shoulder. "Guess I just fancied some exercise." Not my best excuse by any means, but it would have to do.

He drew a noisy breath. "Well, next time, fancy it when I'm not tryin' to catch up."

I scowled. "What do you want?"

"Why do I have to want something? Don't we always walk home together?"

"Oh, yeah," I said, deflating. It was a dumb thing to forget. "I thought you were gonna ask me why I wasn't at church."

"Well, I wasn't," Theo said. "But since you mentioned it, where were you?"

"We have a guest," I said, trying to sound like it was nothing. The closer you stuck to the truth, the more convincing your fib sounded.

Unfortunately, Theo wasn't convinced. "A guest who doesn't go to church?"

I batted that away. "He's a Lutheran, I think, or maybe a Methodist." But these were flat-out lies, so I hurried to get back on track. "Not everyone goes to the First Baptist Church, you know."

"I *know*," he said, rolling his eyes. "Good grief, you're in a mood. Why are you actin' like a ninny?"

I was still trying to come up with a suitable response when the Studebaker roared up to the curb. Theo made a show of choking on the exhaust, but I just stood there staring. It had been a while since Mama had picked me up from school.

"Get in, Ella Mae," she said.

I squinted at the car. The sun was at the perfect angle, so I could only just make out Takuma's silhouette in the backseat.

Theo craned his neck. "Is that—?"

"It's no one!" I replied as I dashed around the Studebaker and hopped into the front seat. Now that Takuma was a real, live human being (and living in St. Jude, no less), it seemed especially dangerous to let Theo in on the secret.

Mama peeled away in a cloud of dirt-colored exhaust, leaving Theo to cough and sputter in the shade of the old walnut tree. He must have found it strange that we hadn't offered him a ride, but he would have found it even stranger to ride in the backseat with Takuma.

Once Theo faded to a speck in the side mirror, I sneaked a peek over my shoulder. Takuma was pressed against the window, his eyes as wide as lollipops. They reflected Mr. Whitman's shiny storefront and the giant sculpture of a Mother Lode revolving on the drugstore's roof.

"What do you think of St. Jude?" I asked.

He looked out the window. "Big."

I looked out the window, too. It had never seemed that big to me, but St. Jude was the only place I'd ever been.

"That's fine, Takuma," Mama said, "but maybe you shouldn't lean against the window."

Amazingly, he leaned away.

I swallowed. "Is this all right? I thought Daddy said we couldn't take Takuma out in public."

"Daddy also said he couldn't borrow Daniel's clothes, and he can't have it both ways." Mama sneaked her own peek in the rearview. "Not that Daniel's clothes would fit."

I made a face. "We're goin' shopping?"

"Don't worry," Mama said. "I won't make you try anything on."

St. Jude only had one department store, an ugly-looking place that shared a wall with Arty's Tavern. It didn't even have a name, just an old sign that said DEPARTMENT STORE in faded black letters. At least it wasn't crowded.

Mama set the parking brake, then climbed out of the car and led us up the steps, which sagged a little to the side. The air that clogged the doorway smelled like Gramps and Gran's attic—dusty and lightly perfumed. Still, Mama plowed into the store as if she owned the place, Takuma hot on her heels. I swallowed one last gulp of air, then dove in after them.

I blinked until my eyes adjusted to the dingy light, but even when they did, there wasn't much to see. A few racks dotted the floor, but they were as spread out as trees in the Mojave, and the shelves on the back wall made me think of Mother Hubbard's cupboard. This wasn't a department store so much as a last resting place for ugly and unwanted goods. I was about to turn around when I spotted Chester.

"Mrs. Higbee!" Chester said. "What brings you to our fine establishment?"

I scrunched up my nose. "I thought you worked at the drugstore."

"Still do," Chester said with his signature smile. "But Mrs. Leavitt lets me work a few shifts here and there during the busy season."

"This is busy?" I replied.

It wasn't until his smile faltered that I understood. Chester had always seemed like a grown-up to me—he'd been running the soda fountain for as long as I could remember—but he was only Gracie's age (or maybe a few years older). Mama said that Chester worked because the war had killed his daddy and his family needed him to help, but it had never crossed my mind that he might need to work *two* jobs.

"So what can I do for you?" he asked. "I'm afraid we're out of ice cream, but we have a few leftover Easter dresses . . ."

He trailed off when he realized me and Mama weren't alone. As he looked Takuma up and down, his mouth wobbled back and forth between a smile and a frown.

"This is Takuma," Mama said before the silence could get awkward (or *more* awkward, anyway). "Takuma, this is Chester."

Takuma didn't bow, and Chester didn't offer to shake hands.

"He needs a new shirt," she continued as if she hadn't noticed. "And since we're here, we should pick up some pants and underwear."

At least that snapped Chester out of it. "Underwear," he mumbled, glancing furtively over his shoulder. Without another word, he retreated to the flimsy curtain marked EMPLOYEES ONLY.

Disappointment curdled in my stomach like a cup of spoiled milk. I'd always liked Chester. He'd always seemed different. Apparently, though, he wasn't as different as I'd thought.

While I watched Chester backpedal, Takuma just stared at the spot where Chester had been standing, eyes down, shoulders hunched, like he was carrying a heavy load. He might not have followed the conversation, but he knew a retreat when he saw one.

I wanted to pat his back and tell him things would be okay, but I couldn't decide if it was more of a truth or a lie, and lying to myself wasn't something I was keen to do. I was still trying to decide when Mrs. Leavitt scurried out from behind the old curtain.

"Anna!" she said delightedly. "How wonderful to see you."

Mama sniffed. "You saw me yesterday."

She patted Mama's arm. "Oh, Anna, you never let me get away with anything!"

"Were you trying to get away with something?" Mama asked.

Instead of answering, she cleared her throat. "Chester said you'd like to buy a shirt?"

At the sound of his name, Chester pushed the curtain back, though he didn't leave the relative safety of the archway. I tried to catch his eye so I could glare at him properly, but he kept his gaze glued to the floor.

Mrs. Leavitt clucked her tongue. "I'm afraid we just sold our last one."

Mama motioned toward a nearby rack, which was

drooping beneath the weight of several dozen ugly shirts. "Well, then, what about those?"

"Oh, you wouldn't want one of those," she said. "They're awfully out of season."

The shirts looked just fine from here, but Mama didn't fight her, just made a beeline for the pleated pants that were hanging on another rack. "Well, then, we'll just buy these and order another of those shirts you mentioned." She checked the waist size on the nearest pair. "I think he'd look nicer in gray, but this brown will have to do. Takuma, will you try—?"

"I'm afraid you wouldn't want those, either," Mrs. Leavitt interrupted as she ripped them off the hanger and tucked them under her arm. "This twill's too coarse for our climate."

Mama threw her arms up. "Is there anything in this whole store that you might let me buy?"

Mrs. Leavitt winced, then mumbled, "No."

Behind her, Chester flinched, though he didn't disagree. On the far end of the store, the only other shopper set a casserole back on the shelf, then darted out the door. Her hat was angled low, so I couldn't see her face, but she was obviously a coward. The door wheezed shut on her heels with a tired sigh.

White-hot anger zigzagged across my field of vision, but luckily, Daddy's boxing lesson had included a few pointers on punching with both eyes closed and one arm tied behind your back. I used Mrs. Leavitt's heavy breathing to triangulate her position, but before I could cock my fist, Takuma touched my arm. When I squinted up at him, he shook his head.

I knotted my arms across my chest. Why Takuma didn't want me to teach her a lesson, I had no idea. She'd ignored him, insulted him, and ultimately denied him pants (albeit pleated ones). But I didn't have a chance to outline these injustices before Mama cleared her throat.

"Very well," she said majestically. "A thousand apologies, Virginia, for burdening you with our business."

"Oh, Anna, be reasonable. I mean, how would it look if we did business with—?"

"Don't say it," Mama said. "I can't stop you from thinkin' it, but I *can* stop you from sayin' it, at least when we're around."

Mrs. Leavitt blinked. "It's what he is."

Mama hooked one arm through Takuma's and took my hand with the other. "He's a human being," she replied as she steered us out the door, "just like you and just like me."

14

The drive home calmed me down, but it stirred Mama up. At first, she only glared and muttered hexes on the Leavitts, but once we passed the post office, she started dictating a letter to the Honorable James P. McGranery, the attorney general. She wanted him to prosecute all the ninnies in St. Jude.

By the time that we got home, Mama was fit to be tied. She took one look at the kitchen, then burrowed into the junk drawer.

"Jed was right," she growled. "We can't just stick him in a suit and pretend that he belongs." She pulled out a meat cleaver, then stuffed it back into the drawer. "He's got to learn how to talk. If he's gonna be a part of this town, he's got to speak for himself."

"That's fine, Mama," I said. "But what does that have to do with ladles?"

"I'm gonna teach him," Mama said, but after taking one look at the ladle, she returned it to the drawer. "But I suppose that 'ladle' might not be a useful word."

Takuma tried to grab it, but I gently closed the drawer.

"Why don't you let me do this, Mama?" It seemed like she could use a breather. "You could make yourself some sweet tea . . . or boil some potatoes. You like boilin' potatoes, don't you?"

Mama squinted at me, then, finally, nodded. "But I expect him to be talkin' by the time I finish my first cup!"

"Come on," I told Takuma. "I want to show you something."

Our backyard in the spring was a magical place. The spring break after Theo and I had celebrated our ninth birthdays, we'd spent most of a morning nailing boards to the oak trees that lined the back of my property. Then Auntie Mildred had caught wind of what me and Theo had been up to and made us take them down. She said that we were lucky we hadn't nailed ourselves to those oak trees, but I hadn't thought we'd been in danger. As soon as Daddy had come home, I'd told him the whole story, and he'd spent the rest of the night nailing the boards back up. He'd probably done it just for spite, but it had made me and Theo happy.

I breezed past Mama's swing and skipped across the grass to the oak trees. At the bottom of the biggest one, I pointed up and said, "Guess I'll see you at the top."

Auntie Mildred seemed to think that girls just shouldn't climb trees, but Mama had more practical advice: make the boys go up ahead of you so they can't see up your skirt. I didn't think that boys were as interested in that as girls seemed to think they were, but I did want to see how he handled the fifth rung.

Regrettably, his climb was nowhere near as interesting as

I'd hoped it would be. Takuma went up, up, up, without faltering once. The fifth rung did give him pause—it spanned the gap between two branches and was set off to the side—but he ended up sticking his boot through the opening and boosting himself to the top.

Grinning, I kicked off my Mary Janes and pulled myself onto the ladder. Shimmying up tree trunks was one of my specialties, so it only took a minute for me to reach the main platform.

"That was impressive," I admitted as I dusted off my skirt, "but you should try doin' it in a dress sometime."

Takuma chuckled softly, and I leaned back against the trunk. Me and Theo had worn the boards smooth years ago, so the wood felt like silk on the backs of my legs. Takuma sat down across from me and dangled one leg over the edge, swinging it back and forth like the pendulum in Gramps and Gran's grandfather clock.

I drew a deep breath through my nose. The air smelled like the ocean on the other side of the hills. "It's nice up here, ain't it?"

Takuma nodded. "Nice."

"You understood that!" I replied. "And you understood that last bit about climbing in a dress!"

He didn't have to respond. His blush gave him away.

"Have you been playin' dumb just to throw Dr. Franks off, or have you really learned English in the last couple of days?"

But apparently, this question was too complex for Takuma,

because his forehead furrowed doubtfully. I couldn't decide whether he looked more confused or more thoughtful, but after a long time, he said, "I like talk."

"You like talking?" I asked.

Takuma nodded eagerly.

I snapped an acorn off a nearby branch. If this conversation was going to be our next lesson, then I wanted to make it an especially good one. I played with the lid—no, the cupule—as I considered what words of wisdom I might share with Takuma. Eventually, I decided on one of my favorite memories.

"There was this one time me and Theo played hide-and-seek in the hayfield. Theo's the boy I was with when you picked me up from school. Now, I know what you're thinkin', but he's not that kind of boy. He's my cousin, that's all, so stop smilin' at me like that." I chucked my acorn at his forehead. "Anyway, we decided to play hide-and-seek in the hayfield. Gracie offered to count, so me and Theo scampered off, but what we didn't know was that Uncle George was about to hay.

"I leaped to my feet as soon as I heard the tractor, but Theo's deathly afraid of sudden noises—and beetles, bullies, and badgers—so when *he* heard the tractor, he curled up in a ball. When Gracie came around the barn, she mouthed, *Where's Theo?* and I mouthed back, *Don't know,* and the blood drained from her cheeks. She started flapping her arms like a duck, but Uncle George had his back turned, so it took her a full minute to catch his attention. Once he turned off the tractor, we fanned out to look for Theo, searchin' row by row and hollerin' his name. When I finally found him, he was covered with snot and blubberin' like a baby, but me and Uncle George cleaned him up with the hose in the barn."

At some point during my story, Takuma had turned toward the Clausens', and I wondered if, somehow, he could see what I'd seen. Could he picture the hayfield, hear the tractor's steady growl, smell the freshly cut hay? Did he know what it felt like to worry about losing someone you loved?

But I didn't know how to ask the question any more than he knew how to answer, so I pretended to duck behind a branch and asked, "Have you ever played hide-and-seek?"

"Caw-coo-wren-bow," he replied, then added quietly, "Caw-coo-say."

It took me a few seconds to realize he wasn't speaking English. "What does that mean?" I asked eagerly.

"Hide," Takuma said.

I shivered despite the warm spring breeze that ruffled the new leaves. The way he said it made it sound more like a memory than a random fact. I wasn't ready for Takuma to remember things about his past. If he remembered how he'd lived, would he remember how he'd died?

15

Me and Takuma practiced English as soon as I got home from school, trading words like baseball cards as we swung our legs above the trees. My words sprouted into stories, but his were more like photographs, isolated sounds that only captured single thoughts. I didn't ask him what they meant or how they fit together, and he didn't explain. I liked to think we both preferred it.

On Tuesday, I decided that we needed a field trip. Our legs were getting tired, and some pictures had to paint themselves.

"I'm takin' Takuma to the pond!" I shouted through the open window in the kitchen.

Mama's face materialized behind the crisscrossed screen. "Stay off the roads!" she shouted back.

Good thing traveling cross-country was another of my specialties.

The pond was on the edge of Uncle George's lower field. He only used it in the summer, when his sheep slept beneath the stars, so the rest of the year, we used it as an impromptu fishing hole. The pier had better fish, but the pond was a nice substitute when Daddy couldn't—or wouldn't—take me.

"You'll like the pond," I told Takuma as I squeezed between the fence posts that separated our yard from the empty field that curved south toward the Clausens'. "Uncle George built his own fire pit, and Robby and Daniel hung a tire swing when they were my and Theo's age."

Takuma nodded dutifully as we hopped over clumps of sage and skirted the ravine that dipped down to Traitor's Creek. I couldn't decide whether it was an understanding nod or just a courteous one, but I didn't stop talking. If he liked listening to me talk, then talk was what I'd do. I was just finishing my explanation of how Traitor's Creek had earned its name, which was much duller than it sounded, when we reached Uncle George's fence.

"This way," I told Takuma as I climbed over the rails. Only lamebrains ducked between them. "The pond's just over here."

Takuma didn't move.

"We're not trespassin'," I said, blowing a string of hair out of my face. "This is Uncle George's land, which means it's practically ours, too."

"Out," Takuma said as he pointed at the fence.

"Well, yeah," I said, "you're out. But I just said you could come in."

He still just stood there pointing.

I sighed. "If Uncle George gets mad, I swear I'll take the blame. But Uncle George doesn't get mad, so it won't be a problem. Well, there *was* this one time, but me and Theo left the gate open—and all of Uncle George's sheep escaped—so we probably deserved it."

He thought about that for another second, then ducked between the rails. I tried not to hold that against him.

"You're gonna love the pond," I said as I led him up the rise that bordered the ravine. "Maybe when it's warmer, we could come back and go swimmin'."

When we finally reached the top, Takuma's eyes widened. I couldn't say I blamed them. The pond looked spectacular. The sky was blue, the clouds were white, and the leaves were that electric green they only got this time of year.

Takuma's eager gaze darted from one end to the other. After turning a full circle, he smiled and said, "Home."

I smiled back. "I think so, too." I kicked off my Mary Janes. "It might be too cold for swimmin', but we can always stick our feet in."

Takuma didn't even glance at me. He was too busy studying the clouds.

"Do you need help?" I asked. "I could untie your laces for you. Daniel always used to untie my laces for me."

He batted that away.

"Suit yourself," I said, trying not to be upset. I dug my toes into the dirt to distract myself. The ground was chillier than I'd expected, but my toes didn't mind. They were tired of being cooped up in those awful Mary Janes.

While Takuma squatted down to inspect a ring of

mushrooms, I sat down on the bank and plunged my legs into the pond. The temperature of the water shocked me—if the ground had been chilly, then the pond was downright frigid—and my immediate reaction was to pull my legs back out. But I didn't want Takuma to think I was a wimp, so I forced myself to keep them in.

"Feels good," I said through gritted teeth. At least they hadn't chattered.

He looked up from his mushrooms just in time to see me wince. I tried to laugh it off, but Takuma wasn't fooled. Still, he didn't back away, just sat down, took his boots off, and dipped his feet into the water.

"Saw-moo-ee," he said, gasping.

"Saw-moo-ee," I replied, rolling each sound around my mouth.

Takuma made a show of shivering. "Saw-moo-ee water," he explained.

I didn't have to make a show. "Yeah, the me-zoo is cold."

Before he had a chance to answer, something tumbled from the trees. It wouldn't be the first time a dead branch had knocked me flat, but it wasn't a dead branch.

It was Theo.

"What are you doin' here?" I asked, jerking my legs out of the pond.

He knotted his arms across his chest. "I could ask you the same thing."

I glared at him, but really, I was more nervous than upset.

There was nowhere to hide Takuma and no way to keep Theo from remembering this run-in. Guess I had no choice but to grab this bull by the horns.

"Takuma, Theo," I said. "And Theo, Takuma."

They didn't dip their heads, just sized each other up.

"So what *are* you doin' here?" I asked to keep the conversation alive.

"Fishin'," Theo said as he offered up his pole. Somehow, I hadn't noticed the line dangling from the trees. "Or at least I *was* until you two came along."

I ducked my head. "I'm sorry. I didn't think anyone was here. We really didn't mean to scare away your fish."

"That may be," he said, "but that's exactly what you did."

I folded my arms across my chest. "Don't get high and mighty, Theo. If you'd told me you were fishin', I would've brought my pole."

"I didn't think you'd want to," Theo said, keeping his eyes trained on Takuma, "seein' as you've been avoidin' me."

I started to say, *I haven't been avoidin' you*, then stopped when I realized that it was partly true. I'd been hurrying home to teach Takuma for the last couple of days. I just hadn't realized that Theo was paying attention.

"Well, I'm here now," I said. "We could take turns with your pole."

"I don't know," he said, digging his toe into the dirt. "I've got some homework at the house."

"I seriously doubt that," I replied. "You don't care about your homework any more than I do."

When Theo hesitated, I wiped my sweaty hands off on my skirt. The stakes were suddenly much higher than they'd ever been before. I could deal with Mrs. Leavitt's snub, and Chester's rejection wasn't unbearable, but I didn't think that I could handle the same treatment from Theo. I just wanted it to be like it had been before, when Theo was the Tonto to my stouthearted Lone Ranger.

"Stay," I croaked like a bullfrog. I hadn't meant to beg, but that was how it had come out. "We can be the Three Musketeers."

Theo's eyes hardened. "We're not gonna be the three *anything*," he said, then thrust the pole into my hands. "Here, you can just have it. The fish ain't bitin', anyway."

My heart felt like it was breaking, but instead of dissolving into tears, I sniffed. "Guess we'll see about that."

It was no secret that Theo was as bad at catching fish as I was at keeping my nails clean. I had no doubt that I could catch one (and likely two or three). I'd even leave myself enough daylight to teach Takuma how to fish.

I expected Theo to leave, but he planted himself on the old log Robby had rolled up to the fire pit and plopped his chin into his hands. I'd wanted him to stay, but not like this. Like he was daring me to fail. At least his doubtful gaze made me more determined to succeed.

It took me a whole hour to catch one pesky fish. Takuma waited patiently, but Theo threw pebbles in the pond every time my line started to shudder. I told him to knock it off, but he pretended not to hear. When I finally snagged an eight-inch catfish, I tugged the hook out of its mouth and chucked it at the ground near Theo's feet. Its death throes muddied his new shoes, and I couldn't help but smile.

"Clean that," was all I said.

Obediently, Theo pulled a Swiss army knife out of his pocket.

I returned my attention to Takuma. "The thing about fishing is that it's all in the wrists." I plopped the pole into his hands. "It really ain't as hard as our poor Theo makes it seem."

But Takuma wasn't watching me; he was watching Theo, who was using his Swiss army knife to strike the match he'd just produced. Uncle George always kept a stash of kindling and split logs by the fire pit, and Theo wasn't wasting any time. As his match flickered to life, Takuma flinched.

"Takuma?" I asked quietly.

Takuma didn't answer. In fact, he didn't even glance at me.

Theo looked up from his tepee of pine needles and twigs, which had just started to smoke. "What's wrong?" he asked Takuma. It was the first thing he'd said to him directly. "Haven't you ever seen a fire?"

Takuma clutched the pole like it was his only connection to this spot, this pond, this life. Except for his bright eyes, which were alive with terror, he looked like a statue.

Theo leaned back on his heels. "I don't like the way he's starin'."

"He's not starin' at you," I said. "He's starin' at the fire."

Theo's little tepee was now fully ablaze. It was steadily

consuming the leaves and bits of grass that had blown into the fire pit since the last time we'd made a fire, weaving trails of sooty smoke. The reds and yellows of the flames were reflected in Takuma's eyes.

"Put it out," I said. A rising wave of panic gripped my chest, but it wasn't mine. It was Takuma's.

"Put it out?" Theo replied. "But how are we supposed to roast your fish?"

A tremor rippled through Takuma's shoulders, reminding me of Sunday morning, when he cowered by the fridge while Daddy went on his rampage. This time, I was brave enough to clumsily pat his back.

"It's gonna be all right," I said. "It's just a little fire. And Theo's gonna *put it out*."

Takuma didn't let go of the pole, but his shoulders did stop trembling. It was something, anyway.

Theo chucked the split log he'd been holding on the fire. "Put it out yourself," he said, then dusted off his hands and retreated down the hill.

"Don't be a numbskull!" I called after him, but he didn't respond. He didn't even turn around.

Muttering hexes at Theo's back, I grabbed the dusty bucket that Uncle George kept next to the fire pit for just such an occasion, then dunked it in the pond and tipped it on the newborn fire. While the flames sputtered and died, I squinted down at Theo, who was now a distant speck at the bottom of the rise.

In the few seconds it took me to dry my hands off on my

skirt, I arrived at my decision. Instead of going after him, I forced myself to turn away. Theo might have needed me, but Takuma needed me more. I grunted as I dragged him to his feet and led him carefully away from the smoldering re-mains. I looked for Theo one last time when we reached the split-rail fence, but he'd completely disappeared.

16

Mama didn't ask us why we'd brought home a dead fish, just fried it up and served it to me and Takuma for dinner. He wolfed it down as if it were the best thing he'd ever eaten, though, of course, that wasn't true. Mama's meat loaf had won a ribbon at the fair for three years running, and she'd already made him that.

When I left for school the following morning, I was surprised to find that Theo was waiting for me by our fence.

"Good morning, Theodore," I said as I breezed through the gate. Mama said that courtesy was the only thing that neutralized scoundrels and conniving kin, and right now, he was both.

"Is that your way of sayin' you don't want to walk to school?" he asked as he hurried after me. "Because if you don't want my company, the least you could do is say so."

I whirled around. "*You* were the one who stormed off yesterday!"

He knotted his arms across his chest. "And *you* were the one who ruined my afternoon up at the pond."

Theo stormed off once again, Lone Ranger lunch box swinging viciously. I would have let him make his exit if we'd been headed opposite ways, but I had no choice but to follow.

"I've said it once," I said as I hurried to catch up, "and I'll say it again if it'll make you act less stupid. I'm sorry we scared away your fish." I folded my arms across my chest. "But I'm not gonna apologize for bringin' Takuma to the pond."

At least that made him stop. "The pond is *our* spot, Ella Mae—yours and mine, Robby's and Daniel's. You had no right to bring a stranger there . . . least of all a Japanese one."

"He ain't a stranger!" I insisted. "His name's Takuma, and he's our guest."

"Where'd he come from?" Theo asked.

"I already told you. From a lab."

Theo looked away. "I didn't think that you were serious."

"Well, of course I was!" I said. "Do you really think I'd lie about something that important?"

"Well, no," Theo admitted. "But I never thought that you'd make friends with a bona fide Jap, either."

I opened my mouth to answer, then snapped it shut again. He made it sound like being friends with Takuma was a bad thing, but Takuma wasn't bad, just different. Or were bad and different the same thing?

"He doesn't belong here," Theo said. "He's not the same as we are, and deep down, I think you know that."

He made another exit, and this time, I let him go. Theo

might have thought that he knew what I believed, but how could he know that when I didn't even know myself?

As soon as I got home, I told Mama about our conversation. I expected Theo's words to plant the same seeds of doubt in Mama's head, but she easily dismissed them. If Takuma didn't fit in with the rest of us, it was only because he'd never had an American upbringing, and bringing up Americans was one of Mama's specialties.

We were halfway through our dinner of waffles and pork links when Mama cleared her throat. Waiting for Daddy to get full on processed pork and maple syrup must have been part of her plan.

"It's time to make a change," she said.

Daddy looked up from his newspaper for the first time in a week. "It took longer than I thought it would, but you've finally come to your senses." He wadded up the *Times* and checked his watch. "If we leave for Pasadena in the next ten or fifteen minutes, I can still make it back in time for *Break the Bank*."

Mama shook her head. "That wasn't what I meant."

He considered that, then shrugged. "You can take him back yourself if you really feel that strongly."

Mama clenched her teeth. "I don't want to take him *back*. I want to take him to school."

Daddy's jaw actually dropped. I lost my grip on my utensils. I'd been about to gobble down my last bite of waffle, but Mama's unforeseen announcement had nearly knocked me flat. It seemed like Mama had just told me that St. Jude wasn't ready for the answers we'd been getting. If they hadn't been ready then, what made them ready now?

Mama fiddled with her napkin. "I know you probably think I'm crazy, but I've given this a lot of thought. What's done is done, and we can't change it. But we *can* give this boy a life, a better life than the one he's had."

"He had a life!" Daddy replied, tightening his grip on his butter knife.

Mama's eyes darkened. "No, Jed, he had a number in some awful man's experiment, and that's no life at all."

Takuma had been eating pork links like they were about to be rationed, but Mama's words made him miss a beat. He didn't look up from his plate, but he did put down his utensils. He'd probably been listening all along, but now he wasn't trying to hide it.

"He had a purpose," Daddy said, "and we should let him get back to it before he can do any more damage."

"What damage?" Mama asked.

Instead of answering, he aimed his fork in the direction of his dealership. "I've sold Greg Leavitt a new Ford every other year for the last twenty, but after you steamrollered his wife at that department store she runs, he's probably never going to buy another car from me again if I can't somehow convince him that that boy doesn't belong to us."

"Well, if he doesn't belong to us, who does he belong to?" Mama asked.

"That crazy scientist!" he said, smacking the only bare spot on the table. The dishes rattled ominously. "We shouldn't have to be responsible for another man's mistake!"

His words nearly bowled me over. I thought Mama had said she couldn't trust him with the truth. When had she broken our pact? The surprises just kept coming.

I must have made a face, because Mama ducked her head. "Don't give me that look, Ella Mae. It's not like *you* haven't told anyone." A single tear spilled down her cheek. "And for the record, I don't think we're responsible for Dr. Franks's mistake so much as the life that it produced. He can rant and rave, but I won't let him have Takuma. If some crazy German scientist brought my boy back to life, I'd hope that *someone* would look after him."

Daddy relaxed a little. "I understand why you're upset," he said as he reached for her hand. "But he won't replace the one we lost."

Mama jerked out of his reach, but before she had a chance to answer, Takuma bolted to his feet. His face was red and splotchy, and as he bowed and mumbled "Are-ee-got-toe," he backpedaled toward the door.

"What's wrong, Takuma?" Mama asked.

"Are-ee-got-toe," he replied. He was less than a foot from the threshold.

When I realized what his intentions were, I yelled, "Takuma, stop!"

It surprised me when he did.

I stuck both hands on my hips. "What do you think you're doin'?"

"Go," was all he said. He wouldn't meet my eyes.

It felt like an unseen hand reached into my chest and squeezed. Renegade tears spilled down my cheeks, but I paid them no heed. I'd thought that I was ready for life to go back to normal, but apparently, I wasn't ready for a life without Takuma. If Theo had planted seeds of doubt, Takuma had plucked them back out. I didn't want him to go away. What if someone awful found him? Or what if someone took him in and he forgot all about me?

"No, you can't go," I croaked.

He dragged a hand under his nose, then sneaked a peek at Mama and Daddy. Daddy unfurled his newspaper with a vicious flick, but Mama smiled back.

"Stay," she told Takuma. "It won't be like this forever."

Takuma smiled shyly, then swiftly went back to his seat. After drying my cheeks off on a towel, I carefully went back to mine. Mama seemed so certain that things were going to get better. I only hoped she wasn't saying that to convince herself.

We left for school in the Studebaker bright and early Thursday morning, so I didn't get a chance to stick my tongue out at Theo, but that was probably just as well. I wasn't ready to see him again, not even through a window.

The mood in the car shifted from anxiety to anticipation, then back to anxiety. If Daddy had blown up at the mere mention of the word "school," then what would Miss Shepherd do when we actually tried to enroll him? At least

Mama had made sure that Takuma looked his very best. She'd found him a pair of pants and an old shirt that had been too big for Daniel, then slicked his hair back like James Dean's. A few bits had escaped the pound of Brylcreem she'd employed, but on the whole, he looked respectable (if a little out of style).

Still, I shifted awkwardly when we pulled up to the school. It was a vast, two-story building whose only match for age or size was the old adobe church. As I climbed out of the car, I felt a bit like Wyatt Earp as he'd scrambled off his horse at that ill-fated corral.

I sneaked a peek at Mama. "You think this is gonna work?"

"There's only one way to find out," she said.

I tightened my grip on my lunch pail. "We *are* right, aren't we, Mama?"

She half smiled, half sighed. "I'm not sure of most things, sweetness, but I am sure of this."

That was good enough for me. I linked elbows with Takuma, and Mama linked elbows with me. Their proximity gave me the confidence to march across the parking lot, but as soon as the door clanked shut behind us, my confidence drained out my toes.

I'd attended the St. Jude School for Boys and Girls for the last seven years, but I'd never been inside at such an early time of day. Somehow, I'd never noticed that the ceilings were two stories high or that it smelled faintly of Clorox, as if the janitor had just cleaned up someone's mess.

Takuma stuck to me like a dead bug stuck to flypaper, but I didn't mind. When he unlinked his elbow and draped his arm around my neck, I hesitated for a moment, then circled mine around his waist.

When we reached the office, Mama opened the door, then froze. Miss Shepherd had clearly spotted us, since she was gawking at Takuma like he was a three-headed sheep. But Miss Shepherd wasn't the only one. Mr. Lloyd was hovering behind her.

As his name implied, Mr. Lloyd was Walter's daddy, with a temperament to match. He must have become a principal because he liked being a bully.

"Good morning," Mama said as she dragged us into the office.

Mr. Lloyd didn't respond, just stared at us over his coffee, which was frozen halfway to his mouth.

Miss Shepherd dropped her folders and grabbed the pen behind her ear. "Good morning, Mrs. Higbee. Is there something we can do for you?"

"Yes, ma'am," Mama said. "I'd like to enroll a new student."

Miss Shepherd's gaze darted to Takuma, then darted away. Mr. Lloyd jolted so violently that his coffee slopped out of his mug, instantly soaking through the pages of Miss Shepherd's steno pad.

Miss Shepherd plucked a form out of her desk. "Then I need his name and date of birth, and if you happen to have a transcript, we'd like a copy of that, too."

When she tried to hand the form to Mama, Mr. Lloyd

intercepted it. "Regrettably," he said, setting his coffee on the steno pad, "the St. Jude School for Boys and Girls is quite full at the moment."

Mama snatched the form out of his hands. "You must have an extra desk somewhere."

Mr. Lloyd snatched it right back and tore it down the middle. "No," he said, "we don't."

Mama rolled her eyes. "He barely takes up any space."

"And his English is improving every day," I said. "In fact, just yesterday, he strung two whole words together!"

I decided not to mention that one of them was Japanese, but apparently, it wouldn't have mattered. Mr. Lloyd wasn't impressed.

"I'm sorry," he said with a fake smile, "but with the new move-ins we've had lately, we simply don't have any room."

"What new move-ins?" I replied. "The last new move-ins were the Higginbottoms, and he died two months later!"

Mr. Lloyd scowled. "Hold your tongue! Hasn't anyone ever taught you not to speak ill of the dead?"

"I don't know," I said. "Hasn't anyone ever taught you not to speak ill of the living?"

Mr. Lloyd set his sights on Mama. "Are you just going to stand there while your daughter says such things?"

"No, I'm gonna stand here until you enroll this boy in school."

Mr. Lloyd stuck out his stomach, which was impressive not just for its size but for its resemblance to an inner tube. "Then you're going to stand there for an awfully long time, because the St. Jude School for Boys and Girls refuses to accept him. We may not have all the resources at the disposal of the city schools, but we pride ourselves on the education we can and do provide, and we can't provide that education if there are *opponents* in the classroom."

"The war's over," Mama said. "Or hasn't anyone told you?"

Mr. Lloyd's lip curled. "Some wars never end."

Takuma might not have understood every word that they'd exchanged, but he knew fighting words when he heard them. Still, he didn't raise his fists, just stuck out his chest. It was even more impressive than Mr. Lloyd's stomach.

Miss Shepherd shuffled through her folders. "There's a colored school in Santa Ana. If you'd like, Mrs. Higbee, I can get the address for you."

Mama raised her eyebrows. "You expect us to drive to Santa Ana when there's a decent school right here?"

Mr. Lloyd grinned wickedly. "You know what they say, Anna—*separate* but equal."

Mama's eyebrows drooped, and Mr. Lloyd's smile turned smug. He obviously thought he'd won, but she was just getting warmed up. Red-hot rage crept up her neck, but just before she blew her lid, Takuma touched her arm. He might as well have pricked her with a pin.

"Well, then," she said, deflating, "I guess we'll just be on our way."

Mr. Lloyd held up his coffee. "We wish you the best of luck."

"Sure you do," she muttered as she headed for the door.

I thought Takuma would go with her, since he was clinging to her arm, but Mama was too quick for him. When he could no longer hold on, he teetered, then went down.

Mr. Lloyd chuckled. "If this is his idea of a protest, he needs to work on his technique."

Mama didn't comment, just grabbed Takuma's arm and helped him to his feet. She pressed her lips into a line as she gave him a once-over, but when I tried to ask her what was wrong, she cut me off with a sharp look.

Mr. Lloyd glanced at his watch. "You'd better take him out the back. I don't want him to scare the children."

"We don't scare that easily," I said, blowing a string of hair out of my face.

Mr. Lloyd just stood there watching, but instead of getting mad, I cringed. A month ago, I might have stared at a Japanese man, too. Now it shamed me to think that I'd ever been that person.

17

I tried to wheedle Mama into taking me home, too, but she flatly refused. My education had to count for two, so I'd better make the most of it. Her declaration was so stirring it almost made me want to try.

After dinner, me and Takuma traded more words in the living room. I would have preferred the peace and quiet of our platform in the trees, but after Takuma took that tumble, staying on solid ground seemed safer.

Or at least that was what I thought until Daddy showed up.

I'd never thought of Daddy as an especially large man, but his surly silence filled the archway. Takuma leaped to his feet as soon as he spotted Daddy, but I folded my arms across my chest and hunkered down in his armchair.

"Did you need something?" I asked.

"*Dragnet*'s on," he said. "Or have you already forgotten?"

"I haven't forgotten," I replied. "But in case you haven't noticed, me and Takuma are busy."

"Well, then, you'd better go and be busy somewhere else, because I'm going to watch."

I stuck out my chin. "We can watch, too, can't we?"

Daddy shook his head. "You heard your mother. No more *Dragnet*."

"But you let me watch two weeks ago!"

"Sorry," Daddy said, "but that was then, and this is now." He picked me up as easily as if I were a feather. "So if you'll take our guest and go, I'd be much obliged."

Takuma headed for the door, but I folded my arms across my chest.

"You can't just send us away. We have rights, you know!"

Daddy's forehead wrinkled, but Takuma said, "Go, Ella Mae."

"No, I won't go!" I said. I meant it to sound obstinate, but it came out like a sob. "I'm the official tuner!"

I expected him to ground me, but he just stood there, almost crying. Daddy never cried, so this was something to write home about, but before I had a chance to ask why his tear ducts were malfunctioning, Mama burst into the room.

"What's goin' on?" she asked. Her cheeks were streaked with flour, and she was carrying a half-made pie crust.

"Daddy's watchin' *Dragnet,* and he won't let us stay!"

Mama's gaze flitted to Takuma, then lingered on Daddy. She must have concluded that his tear ducts were malfunctioning, too, because she rubbed her neck and said, "Ella Mae, just leave him be."

I opened my mouth to argue, but the doorbell cut me off.

Mama motioned toward the entryway. "Please get the door," she told me.

Reluctantly, I got the door. I expected it to be a sales-man—they always had some new elixir that they wanted us to buy—but it was only Gracie. Her gleaming bicycle was propped against our not-white picket fence.

"What are you doin' here?" I asked.

"Hello, Ella Mae," she said, craning her neck to see around me. "I heard about what happened in the office before school, so I thought I'd pedal over and offer my assistance . . ."

She trailed off when Takuma made an overdue appear-ance. Her face flushed red, but not like Daddy's.

"Excuse me," Gracie said. "It wasn't my intention to in-trude. Miss Shepherd made it sound like you were planning to homeschool, and I thought you might be able to use an-other teacher."

I started to close the door. "Sorry, but we don't need your help."

Mama caught it with her foot. "On the contrary," she said, "we need all the help that we can get."

Gracie beamed. "Thank you, Auntie Anna."

"No, thank *you*," Mama said, bumping me out of the way. She drew Gracie into the house and turned her to face Ta-kuma. "Gracie, this is Takuma. Takuma, this is Gracie."

I knotted my arms across my chest. "There's no sense in-troducin' 'em, since they're just gonna ignore each other—"

"Pleased to meet you," Gracie said as she extended her hand.

I gaped at Gracie's hand, but he clasped it in both of his

and pressed his forehead to her palm. They stayed in this position for an uncomfortable amount of time, until I was forced to intervene.

"All right, that's enough," I said.

Mama smiled. "Ella Mae, why don't you fill Gracie in on your teaching methods?"

I checked the living room, but Sergeant Friday was already halfway through his monologue, so I led them into the kitchen.

Gracie sat in Mama's chair. "Which curriculum have you been using?"

I scuffed my foot. "Oh, well, we haven't been usin' a *curriculum*." The word tasted funny in my mouth, like I was eating Miss Fightmaster's lunch. "We've just been tellin' stories, tradin' words."

"Storytelling is an art form," Gracie said, "and there's something to be said for unstructured learning, but if we want proven results, we'll have to use a proven system."

She went on, of course, but I stopped paying attention. I wasn't interested in proven systems so much as being with Takuma, laughing at jokes and telling stories, but something told me that those days were about to be a distant memory.

Gracie came back every day for the next week and a half, plying Takuma with flash cards and homemade gingersnaps. Theo never came with her, and at school, we didn't talk. It was weird to see his sister more than I saw him, but there was no way to avoid it. Theo wasn't of a mind to get to know Takuma, and I wasn't of a mind to leave him alone with Gracie.

At least I had Sunday to look forward to. Gracie had to go to church, so we had the whole day to ourselves. I couldn't wait to teach Takuma how to play marbles.

But Mama had other ideas.

"Get up," she said belligerently as she threw my curtains open, then yanked my covers off.

"But it's Sunday!" I said as I scrambled for my patchwork quilt.

"I know," Mama replied. "We leave for church in seven minutes. And this time, we're *all* going."

"But Daddy said—"

"Yes, Daddy *said*." She wadded up my quilt. "Even parents change their minds sometimes."

I sat straight up in bed, suddenly very interested. "How did you convince him? Did you have to box his ears?"

Instead of answering, she checked her watch. "You're down to six minutes and twelve seconds, so you'd better hop to it."

Ten minutes and two seconds later, we arrived at the old adobe church in our Sunday best (or Sunday borrowed, in Takuma's case). Mama had spent the night altering a pair of Daniel's slacks, but they still exposed an inch of Takuma's socks.

No sooner had I climbed out of the car than I spotted the Clausens, which struck me as unusual. Auntie Mildred always arrived at least ten minutes early. Still, I didn't think much of it, just smoothed a lock of hair down with my spit. Luckily, we'd run out of time to redo my braids.

I pretended not to notice Theo, but as soon as he noticed me, he made a beeline for the door. He only made it a few feet before Auntie Mildred hauled him back. A shiver skittered down my spine that had nothing to do with the cool breeze. I couldn't remember the last time Auntie Mildred had run late or Theo had galloped *into* church. It was practically apocalyptic.

I slid backward a step and peered around the parking lot. And realized the other churchgoers were all peering at *us* like a sea of slack-jawed fish.

"What are they starin' at?" I muttered.

"What do you think?" Daddy replied.

Mama drew a bracing breath, then seized my hand and said, "Come on."

It took all my concentration not to lose my balance as I stumbled along behind Mama, whose sensible black pumps were carving deep tracks in the gravel. I tried to glance back at Takuma, but Mama's pace was unrelenting. It was like she thought the church might blast off to the moon without us.

"Morning, Reverend!" Mama said from halfway across the parking lot. "It's a fine day for a sermon!"

I squinted at the sky, which was dark and threatening rain. The reverend, who was guarding the church steps like a pit bull, knotted his arms across his pin-striped vest.

If Mama was intimidated, she managed not to show it.

"I've been lookin' forward to that lesson on the Good Samaritan all week!"

Reverend Simms's eyes narrowed. I could feel the crowd shifting behind us, but whether they were advancing or retreating, I couldn't have said. When I glanced over my shoulder, my gaze settled on Takuma. He was still trudging up the walk, his dark head bowed as if in prayer. When Mama let me go, I sneaked back to walk with him.

"Did you hear me?" Mama asked. "I said, I've been looking forward to your lesson—"

"I heard you," the reverend said, then tipped his hat at Daddy (who'd been shadowing Takuma).

"Good morning, Reverend," Daddy mumbled.

I hauled Takuma up the steps. "This is Takuma," I told him.

Reverend Simms's lip curled. "Yes, I've heard all about your *guest*."

I felt Takuma stiffen. Was he about to fall again? I tightened my grip on his arm in case he was feeling woozy. It wouldn't help our case if he fell flat on his face.

Mama made a show of glancing at her watch. "Looks like we'd better get inside! Sunday school's about to start."

"You know your family's always welcome at the First Baptist Church," he said, then glowered at Takuma. "But I won't allow his kind to worship in the house of God."

Mama's eyes flashed fiercely. Her rouge looked more like war paint. "You let the Dents in every week. What makes this boy any different?"

"Maleah and her children may be colored, but at least they're not unnatural."

The crowd went perfectly still. Two branches scraped together, and across the parking lot, a baby howled.

"What does *that* mean?" Theo asked loud enough for us to hear.

"It means," the reverend said, "that this so-called *boy* was born of science, not of God. It means he's not a boy at all."

I stuck both hands on my hips. "How do you know what he is or ain't?"

Mama snorted. "Ain't it obvious? Your auntie must have told 'em."

Betrayal coiled in my stomach like a pack of slippery snakes. We'd gone with her to the lab and even rescued her from Dr. Franks, and this was how she'd paid us back, by blabbing our secrets to the neighbors? Auntie Mildred might have been a blockhead, but she'd always been *our* blockhead. Now I couldn't have said whose side she was on.

I rolled up my sleeves. "Did you tell 'em this was *your* idea?"

Auntie Mildred's pale pink hat popped up from behind her car. "I don't know what you mean."

My hands balled into fists, but Takuma shook his head.

"Steady, sweetness," Mama said.

"But she tattled on Takuma!"

"Yes," Mama said, "she did."

"Doesn't that make you angry?"

"Yes," Mama said, "it does."

But she didn't look angry to me. In fact, she looked downright peaceful. Guess it was time to take matters into my own hands.

"So he was born in a lab. Big deal. Just because he came out of a horse pill doesn't mean he's not a boy. He's as good at climbin' trees as any boy I've ever met."

The reverend didn't look convinced.

Mama cleared her throat. "The boy is what he is, and what he is ain't the boy's fault. If the rest of us are good enough to listen to your sermons, then I'd say he's good enough, too."

The reverend made a face. "I guess that's where we disagree."

I threw up my arms. "He's a human being, for Pete's sake!"

The reverend's face flushed purple. "No, he's an abomination, and I won't tolerate his kind in the house of God."

I shrank away from Reverend Simms. I'd never seen him so upset, not even when Mr. Jaeger hurled all over the last couple of pews. He'd just been found not guilty of murdering the foreman he worked for, so he'd spent the night out celebrating with his unruly friends. When he came to church the next morning, Reverend Simms hadn't told him to repent, just dragged him up by his suspenders and sent him back to bed.

Takuma must have rated somewhere below murderers and thieves at the First Baptist Church.

"Then I guess we'll just be lookin' for another place of worship," Mama said, tossing her hair over her shoulder. "Come on, Takuma. Let's go."

She didn't wait for Reverend Simms to reply or Takuma to follow, just dipped her head and whirled around, last year's Easter dress billowing majestically around her ankles. The crowd followed her progress as she marched across the parking lot, but when she climbed into the Studebaker and slammed the door shut on her heels, their eyes flicked back to us. We were still just standing there slouching.

I slid my small hand into Daddy's. It only seemed small when it was nestled in his.

Daddy stared at our hands, then, finally, sighed. "My apologies, Reverend." He glanced up at the clouds. "Looks like we'd better get inside."

The reverend nodded curtly, then shook Daddy's other hand. Daddy tugged me toward the door, but I tugged the other way.

"We can't leave Mama," I said.

Daddy squinted at the Studebaker. "I don't think your mother is planning to come in."

I glanced over my shoulder. I couldn't make out Mama's face, but I could see her arms. They were twisted like a pretzel with too many knots. I drew a shaky breath, suddenly sick to my stomach. I'd never had to choose between my parents before. It was like choosing between my right hand and my left.

Daddy squeezed my hand. "Well, Ella Mae, what's it going to be?"

Indecision made me itch as I looked at Takuma, who was looking back at me with an empty expression. He'd said his first sentence last night (*I like eat pork links*), but if someone asked for his opinion on waffles or orange juice, he wouldn't know how to respond. And if I stayed with Daddy, who would he climb trees with?

"It's gonna be Mama," I whispered.

Daddy drew a shuddering breath as he handed me the keys. "Well, then, you'd better go."

I fell back to the Studebaker on Takuma's arm (or maybe he fell back on mine). Chester refused to meet my gaze, and the Clausens pretended not to know us. Auntie Mildred let me bore a hole through the side of her head, and Uncle George studied the tulips like they were the most interesting things he'd ever seen. And maybe they were. He'd always been a simple man, less prone to shenanigans than the woman he'd married. It really was a wonder that they'd ended up together.

Just before we reached the car, Gracie made her way out of the crowd. "I'm sorry, Ella Mae," she said, though she said it to Takuma.

If she was looking for my mercy, she was going to be disappointed. "You don't have to stay, you know."

She thought about that for a moment, then awkwardly lowered her gaze. She didn't retreat, but she didn't come with us, either.

Mama had already slid into the driver's seat by the time we reached the car. As I climbed into the front, I handed her the keys, which she jammed into the slot. Our tires spit gravel as we roared away, but as we fishtailed onto Robinson, I caught one last glimpse of Daddy. He was still just standing there, not smiling, as a steady stream of churchgoers trudged up the church steps and disappeared into the chapel.

18

I expected Mama to head home, but when we dead-ended into Finch Street, she took a left instead, roaring north toward who knew where like the Devil himself was on her tailpipe.

"I take it we're not goin' home," I said as St. Jude shriveled to a speck in the side mirror. It wasn't quite a question, but it might as well have been.

Mama shook her head. "I take it we're not."

"Then where are we goin'?" I asked.

"To a land of hopes and fears."

I was never going to get half of the things that Mama said.

At least this drive featured cows as well as orange groves and clumps of sage, but we were traveling so fast that the landscape blurred together, streaks of green and black smearing into one another. I'd gotten used to Mama's driving, but from the way that he was swaying, I could tell Takuma needed a break.

"Do we really have to go so fast? Takuma looks like he might hurl."

"Sorry," Mama said as she let up on the gas. "I just don't want to lose my nerve."

"Lose your nerve to *what*?" I asked.

Mama hesitated. "Buy Takuma some new clothes."

For the most part, Mama had left my Sunday schooling to Mrs. Timothy, but there was this one time she decided to teach me the Ten Commandments. As she'd hung the laundry on the line, she'd rehearsed the rhymes with me: "Commandment number one, love the Father and the Son. Commandment number two, don't make statues of your shoes. Commandment number three, don't treat Jesus like a tree."

The rhymes didn't explain what the commandments actually were, but they were just catchy enough that I could remember them. When Mama reached the end, I'd asked her which one was her favorite. Auntie Mildred would have said that all of them were her favorites, but Mama had taken the time to consider her answer. Finally, she'd said, "Commandment number four, enter through the chapel door." When I asked her why, she'd said, "Because I like the Sabbath day. It gives me a reason to put my feet up now and then."

So when Mama pulled up to the Broadway in the middle of Los Angeles, I knew right away that something was horribly wrong. By Mama's own admission, there was nothing more important than honoring the Sabbath day, and shopping at the Broadway had to be against the rules.

Mama dropped the keys into her purse. "Well, there's no sense dillydallyin'."

I craned my neck to see the awnings, which were the color of spun gold, and the rows of shiny windows, seven or eight in all. "Are you sure about this?" I asked. I broke commandments all the time, but Mama's record was still clean.

Mama glanced up at the awnings, then closed her mouth and opened the door. "As sure as I ever am," she mumbled as she climbed out of the car.

Reluctantly, I opened mine. The clouds were thinner here, so tricky shafts of sunshine were sneaking through the cracks and bathing the Broadway in celestial light. But I didn't take it as a sign; I took it as a warning.

I eased the door shut on my heels so as not to draw undue attention. These city slickers didn't know us, but I still felt conspicuous. Would lightning bolts rain down from heaven as soon as we entered the store, or did God work in more mysterious ways?

Me and Mama tiptoed toward the door as timidly as church mice. When she looked one way, I looked the other, and when she looked that way, I looked back. Once we were certain we wouldn't be spotted, we grabbed Takuma's hand and bolted through the door.

The air inside the Broadway wasn't too warm or too cold. Soft music emanated from somewhere high above our heads, and sparkling walkways beckoned to far-off destinations like Stationery, Men's Accessories, and Women's Fragrances. It was like we'd died and landed somewhere between heaven and H-E-double-toothpicks.

"What *is* this place?" I asked.

"A trap," Mama said, but instead of turning tail and flee-ing, she hauled us into the store.

We took a few wrong turns—they should have just called it a half floor instead of a mezzanine—but at last, we found Men's Clothing. I grabbed a pair of pants and was in the process of stuffing them under my skirt when Mama grabbed my wrist.

"Stop that," Mama said, returning the pants to their shelf. "We're gonna do this right, not skulk around in corners like a bunch of common thieves."

I folded my arms across my chest. "If we're gonna do this right, then why'd we come on a Sunday?"

Mama's cheeks reddened, and for a second, I thought she was on the verge of confessing. But then she straightened up. "Because we did, so quit your whinin'."

I felt my cheeks redden, too. Even though these folks didn't know me from Eve, I still felt funny standing out in the open, where God and everyone could see. I was trying to burrow into a rack of briefcases—why I'd gone for the briefcases instead of the silk ties was a mystery—when a deep voice said, "Excuse me."

Me and Mama flinched (though she wasn't the one up to her ears in leather).

If the man thought we looked guilty, he managed not to show it. "Can I help you find something?"

"Yes, sir," Mama said as she straightened back up. "We're just lookin' for a pair of pants. I'm afraid Takuma's"—she gestured in his direction—"are a few inches too short."

The man, whose name tag read CLEVELAND, did a double take when he noticed Takuma. His Adam's apple bobbed as he gave Takuma a once-over. I opened my mouth to give him a piece of my mind, but Mama cut me off.

"If you'll point us in the right direction," she said, "I'm sure that we can manage."

Cleveland fixed his tie. "Most of our pants are in the back." He motioned toward a distant corner. "But if you don't mind my company, I'll be happy to walk you over."

Cleveland took off like a jackrabbit, and we had no choice but to follow. Daddy prided himself on his navigational skills (especially in department stores), but he would have been no match for Cleveland. A prize-winning greyhound probably would have fallen behind.

"Sportswear's over there," he said once he finally stopped. He didn't even look winded. "But I assume you're in the market for something more formal?"

He said it like he'd guessed we usually went to church on Sundays, though it didn't seem like he was judging us. Maybe I could forgive him for eyeballing Takuma like he was from outer space.

"Oh, well," Mama said, "I'm sure he's gonna need more than one. If this pair doesn't fit, the rest probably won't, either."

"Well, in that case," Cleveland said, "let me grab some possibilities."

He then proceeded to show us every pair of pants in the whole store, and Mama proceeded to purchase all but the pink plaid. Next, Cleveland rolled out shirts, then socks, then boxers or briefs (though I averted my gaze for that last one). By the time Cleveland announced that his shift was almost over, Mama had spent more than a hundred and thirty-eight dollars.

I plopped my chin into my hands while she wrote out the check. "You think Daddy's gonna mind?"

"If he does," Mama replied, "I'll tell him I was makin' the most of my one day of sin."

Mama ripped the check out with authority. I thought her hands trembled slightly as she passed it to Cleveland, but her blue eyes were determined.

"Thank you, Mrs. Higbee," Cleveland said as he slid the check into the register, then offered her his hand. "It's been a pleasure doing business."

Mama shook it weakly, then eased a shirt box off the counter and tucked it under her arm. It had taken Cleveland fifteen minutes to box up our purchases, and that had been with LINDY's help. The stack of white boxes was three or four feet across and at least that many high.

"Here," Cleveland said as he rolled out a dolly. Without waiting for permission, he started stacking boxes with the speed of one of Santa's elves.

I just stood there gaping as the stack kept getting higher. Takuma pitched in where he could, but it looked like his leg was bothering him, so he kept taking breaks. By the time that they were done, they'd loaded up two dollies (though I couldn't have said where the other had come from).

Cleveland dusted off his hands. "Can I help you out with that?"

Mama didn't have a chance to answer before Takuma grabbed one dolly and I grabbed the other. It was like we'd planned it.

"No, sir," Mama said. "It looks like we can manage."

"Very well," Cleveland replied. "I hope you have a great day!"

"You too," Mama mumbled, but she didn't sound like she meant it.

I saluted Cleveland, then scurried after Mama, dragging my dolly behind me. My initial concerns about the Broadway had evaporated, so I wanted to look at everything on our way out of the store, from the cowboy boots to the pearl necklaces to the bright yellow lemon puffs. But every time I lagged behind, Mama clucked her tongue, and Takuma bumped my dolly.

After bumping my dolly for what was probably the twelfth time, Takuma asked, "Ella Mae?"

That made me and Mama stop. Takuma didn't usually try to get our attention. He preferred to bide his time until we spoke to him.

He motioned to our dollies. "Race?"

It took me a few seconds to figure out what he meant, but once I got it, I grinned. "Only if you want to *lose*!"

I didn't wait for him to answer, just took off like a firework on the Fourth of July. But my lead was short-lived, since he'd already closed the gap by the time we reached the purses. I expected Mama to intrude, maybe even ground us for having too much fun while we were sinning, but she only hurried to keep up.

I was still a few feet ahead when I spied the front door. Putting on a fresh burst of speed, I barreled around the final turn, determined to reach the front door first. But I only made it a few steps before something crashed behind me.

I ground to a halt, losing control of my dolly. As it careened into a mannequin, the boxes fell at its feet. I didn't take the time to restack them, just scrambled back for Takuma.

I found him lying in a heap at the edge of the walkway, one leg twisted awkwardly underneath him. It didn't look broken (or at least *badly* broken), but from the way that he was wincing, I could tell he was in pain. Daniel had made the same face when he fell off the tire swing and brutally twisted his right ankle. He hadn't needed a cast, but he'd been laid up for weeks.

"What happened?" I asked as I crouched down beside him.

"Trip," Takuma said, then added with a grimace, "Hurt."

"What hurts?" I replied. It was hard to know where to begin.

A single tear leaked out his eye. "Everything," he said.

I crinkled my forehead. That didn't sound like just a sprain. Luckily, Mama showed up before I had to do anything drastic (like cut off his legs).

"What happened?" she asked.

"Nothing," I said. "He just fell."

Mama pressed her lips into a line as she looked him up

and down. I'd gotten used to strangers and mean folks looking at him like that, but not Mama. Never Mama. I wanted
to ask her what she'd seen, why her eyes looked so worried,
but I knew better than to bother her when she was deep in
thought. Finally, she asked, "Can you stand?"

He gritted his teeth and nodded.

"Then let's get you up."

It wasn't a pretty sight, but between Mama and the dolly,
we managed to get him back on his feet. I tried to offer my
assistance, but there wasn't much that I could do. Takuma
outweighed me by quite a few Mother Lodes.

Mama blew a string of hair out of her face. "Will you pick
up these boxes while I get Takuma to the car?"

"Of course," was all I said. Now wasn't the time to be
disagreeable.

"Thank you," Mama said, then led Takuma away.

Just before they turned the corner, Takuma turned back.
"Are-ee-got-toe," he murmured, and even though his cheeks
were pale and his leg couldn't take much weight, he managed a weak smile.

There was that word again. "Does that mean 'thank
you'?" I asked.

He nodded, still smiling.

"Well, I'll be," I said as I sat back on my heels. I'd heard
of old dogs and new tricks, but what about new dogs and
old ones? I'd thought I was the teacher and Takuma was
the student, but apparently, there were a few things that he
could teach me, too.

19

Mama called the lab first thing Monday morning. Luckily, Miss Kendall was able to squeeze us in that afternoon. Mama tried to ship me off to school, promising that she'd take care of it, but I flatly refused. If anyone was going to take care of Takuma, it was going to be me.

It was weird to be back in Dr. Franks's lair. It had only been a week and a few days, but it felt like a lot longer. When we broke Takuma out, I hadn't thought we'd come back. And yet here we were, smack-dab where we'd started. My hands curled into fists.

If Mama felt intimidated, she did a good job of not showing it. She didn't say a word to the first secretary, just flashed her driver's license and steered us toward the silver door. She didn't say a word to the next secretary, either, or the one after that. In fact, she didn't say anything until we ran into Dr. Franks, literally. He was carrying a stack of folders, so he didn't see us coming. The folders tumbled to the floor on impact.

"Mrs. Higbee!" Dr Franks said, like he was happy to see her.

But Mama wasn't fooled. "Oh, don't act so surprised. I set up an appointment with Miss Kendall."

"Yes, Imogene did mention that you'd be dropping by. I'm just surprised you followed through."

While they chatted like old friends (or maybe sworn enemies), me and Takuma grabbed the folders. I couldn't have cared less about Dr. Franks's files, but I didn't want Takuma to pick them up alone.

Dr. Franks fluttered his arms like an anxious mother hen. "Oh, subject oh-one-eight, you really don't have to do—"

"Takuma," I cut in. "His name's Takuma, not 'subject.'"

Dr. Franks opened his mouth to answer, but before he could put me in my place, Takuma tried to stand back up. His leg gave out beneath him, and he crashed back to the floor.

"Takuma!" I said at the same time Dr. Franks asked, "How long has this been going on?"

"Just a few days," Mama said as she gave Takuma a hand.

I looped Takuma's arm through mine. "Maybe he hurt his knee when he fell yesterday."

Dr. Franks pursed his lips. "Perhaps," was all he said, but it sounded like, *I doubt it.*

We dropped Takuma off outside a dressing room, then made our way upstairs. The long, skinny room felt bigger than it had the time before, but then, it was also emptier.

While we waited for Takuma to change out of his clothes, Mama cleared her throat. "It was wrong of me to drag you to the Broadway yesterday." Even though she whispered it, her voice echoed in the empty room. "I wasn't mad at Jesus, but I'm afraid I took it out on Him."

"Who were you mad at, then?" I asked.

"No one," Mama said. "I was just mad at life, I guess."

I didn't have a chance to ask her what she meant before a door opened in the gym and Takuma reappeared. He looked especially vulnerable in that old teal robe, but the assistants didn't seem to notice. They herded him out into the open, oblivious to his shivers or the way he grimaced with each step.

Dr. Franks pushed a nearby button, and the intercom crackled to life. "Go ahead," he said, though he already sounded defeated.

Takuma didn't wait for more instructions, just lumbered toward the balance beam. Each step was so off balance that he looked like he was walking on the side of a hill. Wincing, I looked away. I couldn't bear to wait and see if he took another spill.

"What's wrong?" Mama demanded.

"What isn't?" Dr. Franks replied. "It's a neurodegenerative condition."

"Yes," Mama said, huffing, "but what does that *mean*?"

He refused to meet her gaze. "It means his motor neurons are failing."

"His motor *what*?" I asked.

Dr. Franks's shoulders slumped. "It means his brain is losing control." It sounded like his dog had died.

As if on cue, Takuma tripped over the balance beam. The assistants rushed to help him, but I still felt helpless. He needed me and Mama, not those stiff, unfeeling folks who hid behind their masks. He needed his family.

"Well, there must be something we can do," I said.

Dr. Franks shook his head sadly. "I'm afraid the damage is already done."

Mama's eyes narrowed. "There's something you're not tellin' us." She leaned toward Dr. Franks. "What's really goin' on?"

"Nothing!" he replied as he shrank away from her. "It's just—well, I'm afraid—"

"Don't get your knickers in a bunch." She folded her arms across her waist. "We can't force you to tell us. But if you think we haven't noticed you have something to hide—or something *more* to hide—then you're sadly mistaken."

I expected Dr. Franks to argue, but he just looked away.

"Just tell me this," she said. "Is he gonna end up like President Roosevelt?"

President Roosevelt had died only a few months after Daniel, so I hadn't known him well. But when it came out after his death that he'd spent years in a wheelchair, it had made the evening news. Apparently, he hadn't wanted us to think of him as crippled, but it was hard not to think of him that way. Suddenly, it was hard not to think of Takuma that way, too.

"No, Mrs. Higbee," Dr. Franks said. "If his symptoms

progress predictably, he won't end up in a wheelchair for any length of time."

Mama eyed him like she thought he was one of Auntie Mildred's riddles, but Dr. Franks lowered his gaze, refusing to be solved.

20

Dr. Franks might have been convinced that Takuma's motor things were failing, but Mama refused to take his finding as anything but a somewhat educated guess. We'd spent so long training his mind that we'd neglected the rest of him. He didn't need a wheelchair; he just needed some exercise.

The next day, Mama incorporated a daily workout into his schedule. I volunteered to be his trainer, since I was handy with a stopwatch (or at least I would have been if I'd ever handled one), but when I mentioned this to Mama, she just offered me her old straw hat. Apparently, these weren't going to be those kinds of workouts.

I tried to change her mind, but Mama's decision was binding. A baby had to crawl before it could learn to walk, and Takuma had to walk before he could learn to run. Grudgingly, I took the hat and dragged him out the door.

We walked in silence for a while, both of us lost in our own thoughts. Takuma's leg was doing better—he hadn't fallen once all day—and the air was getting warmer. It smelled like the orange blossoms were just starting to bloom.

I drew a deep breath through my nose, then blew it back out through my mouth. "Do you like oranges?" I asked.

His forehead wrinkled. "Oranges?"

I made a ball out of my hands. "You know, those orange fruits?" But as soon as I said it, I knew he wouldn't understand. I thought about it for a second, then pretended to peel the ball. "You have to peel 'em if you want to get to the segments inside, and the juice runs down your hands, and you have to lick it off."

The peeling must have struck a chord, because he smiled and said, "Orange-ee."

"Orange-ee," I said, trying out the unfamiliar word. "You know, that makes me think—"

I broke off when I realized he was no longer beside me. He was on his hands and knees, clutching the back of his leg.

I squatted down beside him. "Is it your motor things?" I whispered. I didn't want it to be, but it was time to face the facts.

Takuma didn't answer, but whether that was because he didn't know or couldn't speak, I couldn't decide.

I thought about stroking his hair, then immediately thought better of it. According to Dr. Franks, Takuma's motor things were in his brain, and I didn't want to mess them up. "Is there something I can do?" I asked. I didn't like this helpless feeling.

Takuma grabbed a fence post and tried to drag himself back to his feet, but he didn't have the strength. When he pulled his hand away, I noticed a sliver in his thumb. I tried to grab his wrist, but he cradled it against his chest.

"Fine," he said through gritted teeth.

"No, you're not," I said as I wedged my shoulder in his armpit. If Samson could destroy a temple just by tugging on two pillars, I could certainly do this. But when I tried to stand back up, I just didn't have the leverage.

This was the worst pickle I'd ever been in (and I'd been in quite a few). Takuma couldn't walk, and I couldn't pick him up. I probably could have left him while I went and got Mama, but with folks like Mr. Lloyd and Mrs. Leavitt on the loose, that didn't strike me as a good idea.

The growl of an incoming Chevrolet presented a possible solution. I tried to catch the driver's eye by waving both arms over my head, but the numbskull sped right past us without even slowing down. I muttered hexes on his kin as I watched his tailgate shrink to the size of a postage stamp, but it didn't make a difference. He still disappeared in a hazy cloud of dust.

We were still just standing there wheezing when another car turned onto Radley. This time, I locked eyes with the driver, who happened to be Mr. Jaeger. He wouldn't have been my first choice, but I'd take what we could get. It wasn't like he was going to murder us in broad daylight; he obviously took more care than that. But when I waved him over, he just kept right on going. He didn't even have the decency to avert his gaze.

I chucked a rock at his tailpipe, but he was already long gone. And we were still stranded.

Takuma rolled onto his side. He couldn't even sit up straight. "Leave me," he croaked miserably.

"I'm not leavin' you," I said, propping my elbows on my knees. "Heaven only knows who might come along."

As if on cue, a pair of bicycles rounded the corner. I whirled around to meet them, hoping against hope that it was Gracie and one of her many beaus.

But it was Walter. And Theo.

Walter grated to a stop, spitting gravel at our shoes. "Well, well, well," he said as he leaned over his handlebars. "Look what the rat dragged in."

I stepped between him and Takuma. "Leave us be," I said, folding my arms across my chest. "This ain't any of your beeswax."

Theo shuddered to a stop a foot or two behind Walter. He only watched us for a moment, though, before he pedaled off, racing back the way he'd come. I'd long suspected that Theo was a coward, but now I knew for sure. I wanted to spit at his tires, but that seemed like a waste of spit.

Walter popped his knuckles. "On the contrary," he said, nodding toward the Olsens' fence, "destruction of private property is everyone's business."

"We're not destroyin' it," I said, though it was sagging

beneath our weight. But the way I saw it, fences were meant to be leaned on. "As soon as he works out this charley horse, we'll be on our way."

It was a bluff, of course—Takuma didn't have a charley horse any more than I had a black eye—but Walter wasn't privy to that piece of information. Hopefully, he'd take the bait and leave.

Unfortunately, he didn't.

"Well, it serves him right," he said as he spit in our direction. "My uncle Mitch lost his right arm to those dirty, stinking Japs. The doctors had to cut it off when he came back from Okinawa."

I lowered my gaze. "I'm sure he's sorry about your uncle." Takuma had never taken pleasure in another person's pain.

Walter batted that away. "Of course, the reverend thinks that he's not even a Jap." He kicked Takuma in the shin. "You hear that, dirty butcher? The reverend thinks you're nothing!"

Takuma bit his lip, probably to keep from crying out, but I could tell that he was hurting. White-hot anger zigzagged across my field of vision, and my hands balled into fists. It was like that day on the playground, but this time, Mrs. Temple wouldn't be able to intervene.

I struck as swiftly as a lightning bolt, upending Walter and his bicycle in a single move. He whacked himself between the legs, but I showed him no mercy. While he curled up in a ball, I smashed his face into the dirt, then seized a juicy-looking clod and shoved it in his mouth.

"Do you taste that?" I demanded. "It tastes like your filthy words."

Takuma yelled my name, but I pretended not to hear. He was probably going to tell me to leave Walter alone, and I was having too much fun.

I waved another clod in Walter's face. "Do you think you've had enough?"

Walter half said, half choked something that I couldn't decipher.

I smiled wickedly. "I didn't think so, either."

But I didn't have a chance to shove it in his mouth before another bicycle trundled up and a familiar voice said, "Ella Mae!"

Instead of answering, I dug my knees into Walter's back. Gracie might have been my cousin, but she wasn't my mama. She couldn't tell me what to do.

Unfortunately, she disagreed.

"Ella Mae!" she said again. This time, she grabbed me by my collar. "You get off that boy at once!"

I tried to wrap my knees around his stomach and keep him pinned against the ground, but Gracie's collar-grabbing gave Walter the opening he needed. As soon as my weight shifted, he bucked me off his back with a bloodcurdling howl. I came down on my fanny, hard.

While I recovered from the impact, Walter scrambled to his feet with a dark gleam in his eyes. But before he could tackle me on his own terms, Gracie stepped between us.

"Go home," she said to Walter, sticking both hands on

her hips. "And be sure to tell your mama to expect my call."

Walter opened his mouth to argue, then snapped it shut again. He glowered up at Gracie as he retrieved his bicycle and swung a wobbly leg over the seat. I couldn't help but grin as he pedaled gingerly away.

Gracie swatted my fanny. "Stop grinning like that, Ella Mae."

I paid her no heed. I'd grin at Walter however I pleased.

She knelt down by Takuma. "I don't think I can carry you, but I do think I can help. Do you think you can walk if I support most of your weight?"

Takuma closed his eyes as another wave of pain swept over him, but he managed to nod.

"Then let's get you back to Auntie Anna's." She looped his arm around her neck. "We'll stand up on three, okay? Are you ready? One, two, *three!*"

Takuma gasped and Gracie grunted as they struggled to their feet, but somehow, they stood up. Once they were mostly upright, she snaked an arm around his waist, and he sagged against her side. I didn't like how she clung to his belt loop and he didn't shy away.

"I can take him now," I said as I stepped in front of Gracie.

"You're too short," Gracie said, easily sidestepping me. "Besides, if Walter circles back, I don't think he's going to settle for calling you two names again."

I stuck out my chest. "I can handle Walter."

"Stuffing dirt in his mouth isn't handling him," Gracie

said. "And don't think I'm not going to talk to Auntie Anna, either."

True to her word, the first thing Gracie did when we got home was set Takuma on the couch, and the second thing she did was tell Mama the whole story. Mama listened carefully to Gracie's blow-by-blow account, then disappeared into the kitchen without saying a word. She came back with her wooden spoon and a handful of lemon drops.

She whacked me so hard with the spoon that tears sprang to my eyes, then dumped the lemon drops into my hand. Mama said the whack was for stuffing Walter's face with dirt while the lemon drops were for protecting Takuma. She offered some to Gracie, but Gracie waved her off. She was too busy propping Takuma's leg up on a laundry basket and tending to his sliver.

Mama mentioned something about steering clear of Walter, but I was no longer listening. I was too busy glaring at the back of Gracie's head. Takuma was *my* best friend, not hers. I was getting tired of her interference.

On Wednesday, I dodged Walter like a bad case of the flu, but there was nothing I could do about dodging Theo. From the way that he kept trying to capture my attention, I could tell he had something to say, but I wasn't in the mood to hear him out. Unfortunately, he tracked me down while I was headed home from school. That was what I got for sticking to the roads.

I stuck up my nose. "I'm not speakin' to you, Theodore."

"Why, because you don't like losin'?"

"No, because I don't like talkin' to Walter's pea-brained friends!"

Theo's smile faded. "I'm not Walter's friend," he mumbled.

I laughed, not very nicely. "Well, you could've fooled me."

He dragged a hand under his nose. "I'm not Walter's friend, all right? We've just been passin' time. It turns out that Walter doesn't have many friends, either."

This was news to me, but I wasn't about to encourage Theo. "I'm not interested in Walter's social life."

Theo stuck his chest out. "Well, *I'm* not interested—"

"In being Takuma's friend, I know."

Theo ducked his head. "It's not what you think," he whispered. "And I really am sorry about what happened yesterday."

"I'm sorry, too," I said. "But then, I should have realized that you were a coward."

It was an awful thing to say, and as soon as I said it, I wished I could take it back. Takuma wouldn't say things just to hurt people. He only said things that were important.

I expected Theo to dissolve into a puddle of snot, but he managed to surprise me. "I did go and get Gracie."

"Yes, you did," I said. "But I didn't need Gracie. I just needed *you*."

Theo made a noise that sounded like a sob, and I lowered my gaze. I didn't want to watch him blubber. Before he had a chance to really get going, I took off my Mary Janes, tucked them under my arm, and darted away with no warning. My stockings were going to look like they'd been through a war zone, but at least I wouldn't have to help him mop up all his snot. When I reached the picket fence, I didn't bother with the latch, just hopped onto a rock and leaped over the gate.

But Theo wasn't giving up.

"I'm not as brave as you," he said as he sprinted up the lawn behind me, "but maybe I will be someday. Maybe I'll stand up to Walter." Under his breath, he added, "Maybe I'll even be *his* friend."

I didn't have to ask who *he* was; Theo obviously wasn't talking about Walter anymore. An unexpected lump lodged in my throat, and I wanted to thank Theo, but I'd already reached the kitchen. And just like that day at the lab, I saw three things all at once:

First, Gracie had beaten us home.

Second, she was kissing Takuma.

And third, he was kissing her back.

21

I shrank back against the doorjamb. I couldn't catch my breath. Theo was pounding up the steps, but I was too busy hyperventilating to even think about blocking his view. When he skidded to a halt, I knew he'd spotted them. He opened his mouth to say something, but the only thing that came out was a funny-sounding gurgle.

At least it alerted Gracie and Takuma to our presence. They sprang apart as quickly as a pair of startled rabbits. Their faces were as red as cherries, and their lips were wet and swollen. But before either of them could explain, Theo turned tail and fled.

"Theo!" Gracie said.

I didn't try to catch him, just hugged my arms around my waist. This was my kitchen, my house, but I suddenly felt like an intruder. I couldn't look at Gracie or even Takuma. Just the sight of them was enough to make my stomach clench.

Gracie cleared her throat. "I'm sorry, Ella Mae. We didn't mean to cause a stir."

At least that made my blood boil. "Then what did you

mean to do?" It was easier to meet her gaze when I was angry.

Impossibly, Gracie's face got redder. "I just wanted to give Takuma another set of flash cards, and when he offered me a cookie, one thing led to another, and we just . . ."

Gracie trailed off when she got to the uncomfortable part, but I wasn't about to make this any easier on them.

"You just *what*?" I asked.

Gracie ducked her head. "Well, what did it look like we were doing?"

I glanced at Takuma (who was glancing at me), but I couldn't hold his gaze. "It looked like you were kissin'," I mumbled at the floor. I didn't mention the fact that he was Japanese, but I was certainly thinking it.

Gracie must have been thinking it, too, because she arched an eyebrow. "And what's so wrong with that?"

I opened my mouth to answer, then changed my mind at the last second. The truth was, I didn't know. Auntie Mildred liked to tell that story about the bird that loved the fish, but I'd never really understood it. Up until this moment, I hadn't needed to.

Gracie must have noticed my bewilderment, because she answered her own question: "There's nothing wrong with it."

"Then why'd you spring apart when you saw me and Theo?"

Instead of answering, Gracie exchanged a loaded look with Takuma. I knotted my arms across my chest. I didn't like the thought that they could have an entire conversation with nothing but their eyes. But before I had a chance to recapture his attention, one of the upstairs doors slammed shut.

Gracie knelt down in front of me. "You can't tell *anyone*," she whispered, her peppermint breath warm on my cheek, "not even Auntie Anna."

"But I thought you said it wasn't wrong."

Gracie's blue eyes turned to ice. "It shouldn't be," she said as she took hold of my shoulders. "It *shouldn't* be, you understand?"

Gracie's gaze was so intense that I wanted to go along with it, but how could something be wrong and right at the same time?

"You have to do this for me," Gracie said, digging her nails into my shoulders. "You have to do it for Takuma."

I tried to wriggle out of her grip, but it was as tight as a bear trap. Behind her, the stairs creaked a feeble warning as Mama barreled down them. When Takuma stepped between me and Gracie and the archway, my stomach did a somersault. Here I was, thinking about handing him over to the mob, and there he was, getting ready to defend us to the death.

I sighed. No matter what I thought of Gracie, I couldn't give Takuma up. He was better than the rest of us combined— and more importantly, he was my friend.

"All right," I finally muttered.

Gracie's eyes defrosted.

"But I'm not doin' it for you."

Gracie half smiled, half frowned. "Thank you, Ella Mae." She scrambled to her feet.

Gracie was still straightening her hem when Mama appeared in the archway. "I found a few more of those picture books!" She stopped short when she spotted me. "Oh, Ella Mae, you're home."

"And just in time," I muttered.

She didn't acknowledge my comment, just sized Takuma up. "Are you feelin' all right, sweetness? You look a little flushed."

Takuma nodded. "Fine."

She stuck both hands on her hips. "Have you gone on your walk today?"

I grabbed his arm. "I don't think so." Finally, I had a chance to get him away from Gracie.

"Maybe you should go with them," Mama told her. "Heaven only knows what would've happened last time if you hadn't shown up."

"No!" I said despite myself.

Gracie cleared her throat. "I think Ella Mae means that she can handle it."

Mama raised her eyebrows. "Is there something you're not tellin' me?"

Gracie forced a nervous chuckle. "Oh, I was just telling Ella Mae that I have some algebra to finish." She waved the picture books weakly. "We can read these when they get back."

I resisted the urge to smack my forehead. Gracie might have been a decent kisser, but a liar she was not.

Mama studied Gracie's face, then, finally, said, "In that case, Ella Mae can read with him. You won't mind a day off, will you?"

Gracie forced a smile. "Of course not, Auntie Anna."

I smiled, too. "My pleasure."

Just like I'd promised, I didn't tell anyone about the possibly-inappropriate-but-definitely-disgusting kiss. So when the rest of the sixth grade was talking about it the next day, I didn't even have to pretend to be outraged.

I heard the first whisper while I was jumping rope at recess. Gordon, Chester's brother, specifically said the word "kiss," and kisses were usually the last things on Gordon's mind.

"Who told you?" I asked, ripping the half-eaten apple out of his mouth.

"Catherine," he replied without skipping a beat. "Now can I have my apple back?"

Grudgingly, I returned his apple, then went in search of Catherine, the daughter of the town gossip. She gave her source up just as easily, and before I knew it, I'd tracked down half of the sixth grade and wound up exactly where I'd thought I would—at Walter.

I found him on the playground as soon as school was over. He was preaching to his choir from the middle of the merry-go-round, which a couple of his minions were turning in a slow circle.

"—must have been awful," he was saying, puckering his lips. "I mean, can you imagine how it must have *looked*?" Walter shook his head. "No wonder he started to hurl."

I pushed the Timothy twins out of the way. "Beat it, blockheads," I muttered.

When they glanced over their shoulders, their eyes bulged at the sight of me. Rusty grabbed Rosy's arm, but she refused to budge. After whispering something in her ear, he turned tail and scampered off.

I didn't have time to fuss with Rosy, just leaped onto the merry-go-round like it belonged to me. "Shut your trap!" I yelled at Walter with all the righteous indignation I could muster.

He must have recognized my voice, because he actually flinched. I stuck both hands on my hips, but by the time he turned around, he'd already recovered. Guess it had occurred to him that he was back on Mrs. Temple's turf.

"Well, look who it is," he said. "I've been wondering when you'd show up."

I resisted the urge to grab his shirt. "How'd you find out?" I demanded.

Walter's smile froze my insides. "How do you think?" he asked as he gestured to a lonely figure huddled under the slide.

His hands were in his pockets, and his shoulders were

hiked up to his ears, but I would have recognized my cousin from a mile away. I probably should have realized that Theo was the source, but that realization still made my heart hurt.

I shoved Walter aside, though I was less upset at him than I was at myself. The crowd parted before me as I jumped off the merry-go-round and slogged toward the slide. The sand sucked at my feet, making it impossible to stomp, but Theo still flinched at my approach.

The crowd bounced up and down, obviously eager for a fight, but I just stood there waiting. The wind whipped my braids around like miniature lassos, and yet I still managed to pretend that they weren't there.

"Is it true?" I finally asked.

Theo didn't bother to answer, but his silence said enough.

Red-hot rage crawled up my neck, coloring my field of vision. My hands clenched into fists, and it was all that I could do not to punch him in the nose. I wouldn't mind bruising my knuckles so long as Theo explained why he'd sold his sister out. But I forced myself to resist. If Takuma hadn't wanted me to box Mrs. Leavitt's ears, he probably wouldn't want me to box Theo's, either.

After a while, the crowd wandered away. We probably weren't being interesting enough. Theo waited until they disappeared, then dipped his head and headed off in the opposite direction. The head-dipping unnerved me. It was like he was turning into Gracie.

174

"Theo!" I called after him. When he didn't stop, I tried again: "Hey, Theo, wait for me!"

At the corner of the football field, Theo finally stopped, though he didn't turn around.

I hurried to catch up. I expected him to say something— to defend himself—but when he didn't, I croaked, "Why?"

He just stood there slouching.

I spun him around. "You can't keep ignorin' me!" But I said it to his forehead, since he wouldn't meet my gaze. "I thought we were friends again."

At least that snapped him out of it. "We *were* friends," he replied, ripping his arm out of my grip.

I stuck out my chin. "You keep makin' it sound like I wanted this to happen, but the fact of the matter is, I don't like it any more than you do."

"Maybe not," he said. "But you wanted him to come."

I narrowed my eyes. "I'm not gonna apologize for bringin' Takuma to St. Jude."

"Well, maybe you should. If you hadn't brought him here, none of this would've even happened."

"Well, if your mama hadn't tried to bring Robby back to life, we wouldn't have had to bring him here!"

Theo stuck his chest out. "Well, if he hadn't killed my brother, she wouldn't have had to bring him back to life!"

I rocked back on my heels. What could I say to *that*?

Theo seemed to know he'd won the argument. He turned around and walked away, and this time, I didn't stop him.

Me and Theo might have argued about the importance of whipped cream (he was for; I was against) and which comic strip was the best (he said *Beetle Bailey*; I said *Dennis the Menace*), but we'd never found ourselves on different sides of right and wrong. I didn't like the way it felt. And I didn't like not knowing which side I was on.

22

That night, I was passing Mama's meat loaf when four knocks landed on our door. They caught me so off guard that the meat loaf flipped out of my hands and landed on its ketchup side. I couldn't look at Mama as I returned the now-empty plate to the table, but she didn't get upset, just dabbed her mouth with her napkin.

"Would you get that, Ella Mae?" she asked.

So she was going to deliver me to the monster at the door. It was no less than I deserved for ruining the meat loaf.

"Yes, ma'am," I mumbled dutifully.

Takuma tried to follow, but Mama shook her head.

"Stay here," she told Takuma, taking a swig of her sweet tea. "I think it will be best to have this conversation in the kitchen. Heaven only knows it's harder to be discourteous when there's a centerpiece present."

It was like she already knew who was at the door and why, but she always seemed to know more than the rest of us did. Takuma hesitated, then, reluctantly, sat back down. Daddy didn't bother to look up from the *Times*.

I tiptoed into the entryway, since I didn't want our caller

to know that I was coming. I'd barely turned the knob when he pushed the door open from the outside. I tensed myself for an attack, but it wasn't a monster. It was Uncle George.

"I want to speak to Jed," he said before I had a chance to greet him. He had neither coat nor hat, and his eyes were as wild as a rabid dog's.

"Daddy's in the kitchen," I replied, sneaking a peek over my shoulder, "but Uncle George, maybe you shouldn't—"

"*Don't*," he interrupted, pushing his way into the house, "try to tell me what to do."

I shrank back against the coatrack. I'd never seen Uncle George like this. He was usually the calm one.

"That unnatural Oriental put his unnatural hands on Gracie, so I'm going to speak to your father whether you like it or not."

I drew myself up to my full height. "Listen, Uncle George, I don't like the fact that they were kissin' any more than you do, but it doesn't seem like you're in any condition to talk sensibly."

Uncle George's nostrils flared. The muscles in his neck stood out like cords. He hadn't acted this upset when me and Theo let the sheep out, and it had taken him three days to track the last of those ewes down. When he raised an open hand, I curled my arms over my head, but before he had a chance to slap me, a shadow fell across our feet.

Takuma's silhouette was straight and tall. He was probably leaning against the doorjamb. "Mr. Clausen," he said slowly. "Leave Ella Mae alone."

Slowly, very slowly, Uncle George twisted around, but before he finished twisting, Mama showed up on the scene.

"Let me through," she said.

For once, Takuma didn't listen.

"I said, let me through!"

But Takuma didn't budge.

Uncle George advanced on him. His steps were slow and careful, but I'd seen him butcher sheep, and he did that carefully, too.

"Let's not be hasty," Mama said. He must not have fooled her, either. "No one really knows what happened. Cathy McConnell filled me in, and we both know she's as reliable as a starvin' cow."

Uncle George pointed at Takuma. "He knows exactly what he did."

"He didn't do anything," I said. The last thing I wanted to do was watch Takuma get his brains bashed in. "Or at least he didn't do anything that Gracie wasn't willin' to do, too."

This time, Uncle George didn't give me any warning, just backhanded me across the cheek. Or at least that was what it looked like he was going to do. I closed my eyes before his hand made contact.

But the contact never came.

The sound rattled my teeth, but I didn't feel the blow. Cautiously, I opened my eyes. Somehow, Takuma had jumped between us despite his lingering limp. His arm had borne the brunt of Uncle George's rage.

"Not Ella Mae," Takuma said.

Uncle George gritted his teeth, but instead of striking him again, he peered into Takuma's eyes. It was like he was trying to catch a glimpse of Takuma's immortal soul.

We were all just standing there, listening to our hearts beat, when Daddy wandered into the room. "There's no fighting in the house, so I'm afraid I have to ask you two to take this mess outside."

"No!" I said despite myself. If they took this mess outside, I doubted Takuma would come back.

Uncle George's eyes flickered to Daddy, then swung back over to Takuma. Finally, they landed on me. I wasn't sure what he was looking for, but the hardness of his gaze was enough to make me flinch.

"That won't be necessary," he replied as he fumbled for his hat. When he remembered he wasn't wearing one, he turned to leave, then turned right back. "But if you *ever* come within a hundred feet of my Gracie again, I swear I'll skin you alive."

Takuma clenched his teeth, but at least he managed not to deck him.

Uncle George yanked open the door and melted back into the night. As soon as the door thumped shut behind him, I grabbed Takuma's arm. His skin was red, not bruised, but when I probed the spots that were the reddest, he still made a face.

I checked to see what Mama thought, but it didn't look

like she'd noticed. She was too busy glaring at Daddy (who'd gone back to reading his *Times*).

"Really, Jed?" she asked. "Your contribution to this near-disaster was to ask them to *go outside*?"

Daddy calmly turned the page. "I thought you were the one who didn't like boxing in the house."

Mama scowled at nothing in particular. "If you thought George was gonna box him, then you need to get some glasses."

I was halfway past the Richmonds' on my way home the next day when a bicycle bell dinged behind me. At least it wasn't Walter. After last night's near-disaster, I'd promised myself that I was never going to hit anyone again, but if Walter picked a fight, that was going to be difficult.

Gracie's cheeks were red and splotchy, and a random clump of hair was dangling from her French twist. For the first time in a long time, she looked like the old Gracie, the one who'd played hide-and-seek with me and Theo and sneaked us snickerdoodles. So when she hollered my name, I didn't even try to run. Gracie might have caused this mess, but the least I could do was hear her out.

When she finally caught up, she tipped off her bicycle. "Thanks for—waiting for me," Gracie said between heavy gasps for breath.

"Are you all right?" I asked.

"I'm fine," she said, waving that off. "I just wanted—to

tell you—that Mama says—I can't come over." She drew a noisy breath. "And Daddy says that if I get within a hundred feet of Takuma—"

"He'll skin him alive."

Gracie flinched. "Did Theo tell you?"

I shook my head. "We're not on speakin' terms."

"I'm sorry to hear that," Gracie said, then sent me a side-ways glance. "It's not because of me, is it?"

"No," I said, sighing. "It's because of Takuma."

Gracie flinched again. "You need to know," she said as she lowered her gaze, "that I really wasn't trying to take Takuma from you."

I felt my cheeks get hot. "I really don't know what you mean."

Gracie sneaked a peek at my beet-red face, and I thought I might explode. I wasn't of a mind to talk about boy things, least of all with her.

But instead of pushing me to say more, Gracie glanced down at her toes. "I'm sorry I brought it up."

"I'm sorry, too," I said.

She climbed back on her bicycle. "I'd best be getting home." Her eyes flickered toward the Richmonds'. "I've al-ready lingered too long."

I followed her gaze. "You don't think Chester's home, do you?"

"Of course not," she replied. "He's at the drugstore until eight."

Chester had known Gracie's schedule for as long as I

could remember, but I'd never realized that she also knew his.

"Do you *like* Chester?" I asked.

"How I feel about Chester is hardly relevant," she said.

That meant yes, of course. "Then why'd you kiss Takuma?"

Gracie blushed and dropped her gaze. "I didn't mean to kiss him. It was one of those things that just happen." She looked me in the eyes. "But I don't regret it, Ella Mae. You understand that, don't you? I don't regret it in the least."

I didn't understand it, but then, I didn't understand kissing, so maybe that explained it. Still, I nodded vaguely so Gracie wouldn't bumble on.

She turned her bicycle around. Guess she was taking the long way. "You'll help Takuma with his lessons?"

"Of course I will," I said.

"And you'll bake a cake for his birthday?"

"It's his birthday?" I replied.

Gracie nodded. "May sixteenth. We're not sure how old he'll be—neither of us could decide if we should count the years that he was dead—but the candles aren't important."

I'd always thought the candles were the *most* important things, but maybe you stopped counting birthdays at the ripe old age of sixteen.

"I knew I could count on you." Gracie tried to smile, but she was obviously trying not to cry. "I guess I'll see you around."

"No, I don't think you will," I said.

"Yeah, I guess you're right." She swept the clump of hair

out of her face, but it looked like she was actually wiping off a tear. "Tell him good-bye for me."

"All right," I said uncertainly. Maybe I was missing something, but that seemed kind of extreme. Auntie Mildred couldn't keep her under lock and key forever, and if I had anything to say about it, Takuma wasn't going anywhere.

23

When I got home, I found Takuma hovering over one of Daniel's sketchbooks. Daniel had owned hundreds, so they were hard to keep track of, but as I inched closer to Takuma, I could tell that this was Daniel's last. It had come back from Belgium with his other personal effects. Mama had found it in her closet while she was digging out those picture books, and Takuma had asked if he could keep it. I wasn't sure if he was using it for writing or for drawing, but he'd been dragging it around all day, scribbling in it feverishly. At least he looked up when I came in.

"Looks like it'll just be you and me," I said, since I didn't want to get his hopes up.

I expected him to frown or maybe burst into tears, but he only glanced at the books Mama had left on the end table like he wasn't sure what to do with them.

I sat down beside him. "I can read 'em with you, if you want." I tried not to sound too eager.

"Yes, ma'am," Takuma said as he set his sketchbook down.

Biting my lip to keep from smiling, I retrieved one of the books. It looked like a collection of illustrated Bible stories.

"I remember this!" I said as I flipped through the pages. "The old reverend gave it to us when I was just a baby." I flipped back to the beginning and read the first title out loud: "'How the Lord created the heavens and the earth and the first human beings.'"

Takuma sat up straighter, but instead of reading more, I tossed the book onto the couch. I wasn't interested in finding out how God had made Adam and Eve. It probably involved a giant horse pill.

"Okay?" Takuma asked.

I plopped my chin into my hands. "Have you ever read the Bible? Not these stories for babies, but the real, actual Bible?"

Takuma shook his head.

"It's chock-full of awful stories about folks doing awful things. There's this one about two brothers, Cain and Abel. Cain's a farmer like Mr. McConnell, and Abel's a rancher like Uncle George. Anyway, the Lord commands them to make an offering, so Abel offers a sheep, but Cain offers an orange."

Takuma leaned forward in his seat, his eyes as wide as silver dollars. It was too bad that the reverend had forbidden him to go to church. Mrs. Timothy would have appreciated an eager student for a change.

"I don't know a lot about offerings," I admitted, "but apparently, the Lord likes sheep more than He likes oranges. When He accepts Abel's offering instead of Cain's, Cain gets really mad. The Lord tries to explain, but Cain doesn't want to hear it. He goes to Abel's ranch and kills him in cold blood."

Mrs. Timothy always told us to put ourselves into the scriptures, to make the stories about us, but I'd always considered that to be the most useless thing I'd ever heard. What could I have in common with someone who'd walked and talked with God? But for once, I understood what she'd been trying to tell us. Apparently, Mrs. Timothy had finally gotten something right.

"I've always thought that Cain was stupid. I mean, why did he think he could get away with murder when he saw God every day? But the truth is, he doesn't seem quite as stupid anymore." I drew a shaky breath. "I might not have killed my brother, but in lots of ways, I'm just as jealous."

Takuma didn't ask me to explain, and I was happy not to have to. Maybe it was because he didn't understand the words, but I thought it was because being kind was just his way.

I dragged a hand under my nose. "Does that make me a sinner?"

He considered that, then shook his head. "No, Ella Mae is friend."

I sniffed. "That's mighty kind of you."

Takuma bowed, and in a way, it felt like we were back at the beginning—but the beginning of what?

A few nights later, I woke up to the sound of someone retching. I'd been dreaming about Daniel drawing pictures in the sky, so it took me a few seconds to break the surface of the dream. Then I heard it again and suddenly woke up. I raced into Takuma's room, but Mama was already there.

"Go back to sleep," she told me.

"What's wrong with him?" I asked.

"He'll be fine in the morning."

Even half asleep, I could tell that she was lying. "What's wrong?" I asked again.

"Nothing you can fix," she said. "Now go back to sleep."

But I didn't go back, just lingered by the door. Mama had left the hall light on, so my outline cast a shadow across the bed, the rug, Takuma. He looked so small and pale beneath Daniel's patchwork quilt. I wanted to protect him, but just like Mama had said, there was nothing I could do.

"Mama?" I bleated like a lamb. I didn't like this helpless feeling, but it wouldn't go away.

She hauled herself back to her feet and wrapped her arms around my shoulders. "It'll be all right," she murmured. Her breath tickled my ear. "I promise I'll look after him."

She pressed her lips against my forehead, then nudged me out the door. This time, I didn't argue. Takuma was retching again by the time I reached my bed, but Mama had promised she'd look after him, so he was going to be fine.

Or at least that was what I told myself.

It was harder to believe as I lay in the dark, alone, one hand pressed against the wall that separated me from him. I wished that he could fall asleep and feel better in the morning. I wished that I could, too. But sleep was hard to come by when the folks you loved were hurting.

When I woke up the next morning, my hand was still pressed against the wall. I couldn't remember falling asleep, but I must have at some point. For a long time, I just lay there, staring up at the ceiling. Trying to convince myself that Takuma wasn't really sick. But when I went down for breakfast, he looked like a walking corpse. Though he brightened at the sight of me, I was nowhere near fooled. He only took two bites of oatmeal before it came back up.

I worried on my way to school, during Miss Fightmaster's lessons, and on my way back home. What if Takuma wasn't fine? What if this wasn't the flu? These questions gnawed my brain like a dog chewing a bone. By the time I hurtled through the door, I was ready for some answers, but Mama wasn't available. She was on the telephone.

"Where's Takuma?" I asked, anyway.

She pressed a hand over the mouthpiece. "I think he's takin' a nap."

"Has Dr. Olsen been to see him?"

Instead of answering, she turned around. "Yes, ma'am," she told the operator. "I'd like to place a call to the Japanese embassy."

I'd never heard of embassies, let alone a Japanese one, but if she thought that would distract me, she was in for a surprise. While she twiddled Daddy's fountain pen, I retrieved a shriveled apple and hunkered down to wait.

The apple kept me busy—I had to eat around the bad parts—so I didn't pay attention to Mama's conversation. When she chucked the pen at the refrigerator (and the telephone a moment later), I came to the conclusion that it hadn't gone well.

"What's the matter, Mama? Did the embassy not want to talk?"

"Oh, they wanted to talk," she said. "They just wanted to talk about a bunch of things they must have known I couldn't talk about."

"What kinds of things?" I asked.

She reeled the telephone back in and returned it to its hook. "Oh, just where Takuma came from. How he ended up in California." She chewed her pinky nail. "I might have been able to remember the name of the town where he was born, but I couldn't explain how he ended up here."

I scrunched up my nose. "But why did the embassy want to know that stuff?"

Mama looked at me, then looked away. "So they could send him home."

I narrowed my eyes. "I thought he *was* home," I replied.

"He can't stay here forever." She flipped a braid over my shoulder. "He doesn't belong here, Ella Mae."

I jerked out of her reach. If she was going to say things like that, I didn't want her to touch me. "You told Daddy he belonged. And you promised me you wouldn't take him back to Dr. Franks."

Mama rolled her eyes. "I'm not gonna take him *back*. But I would send him home." She pressed her lips into a line. "He had a family, a life, and maybe they're just what he needs to fix these damaged motor things."

I pressed myself into the corner, suddenly desperate to escape. "What are you tryin' to say?"

Mama cupped my cheek. Her hand was rough but also warm, like the boards in the oak trees before we wore them smooth. "What I'm tryin' to say is that, if a war took you away from me and a crazy scientist brought you back, I'd want you to come home."

I blinked back angry tears. "But I thought you loved Takuma."

"Of *course* I love him," Mama said as a single tear dripped down her cheek. "But that's why we have to let him go."

24

All afternoon, I thought about what Mama had said. If we really had to send him home to prove how much we loved him, then that was what we'd do. But it was a long way to Japan, and maybe he'd rather save the trip. What if he didn't remember his old life? What if me and Mama were the only family he knew?

There was only one way to find out.

Mama had tried to feed him dinner in his room, but Takuma had insisted on eating dinner at the table. Now he was holed up in the living room, hunched over his sketchbook. I approached with cautious steps, since he didn't look terribly steady. When I finally got close enough to see what he was working on, my elbow bumped his arm.

"Oh, I'm sorry!" I said. The gash was seven inches long and not easy to erase. Daniel hadn't let me get within five feet of his drawing hand, but I'd only just remembered that.

Thankfully, Takuma didn't scold me. In fact, he hardly seemed to notice. After studying the gash, he incorporated it into his drawing.

I licked my lips. "May I sit down?" I couldn't have said

where this formality had come from, but for some reason, it felt right.

Takuma blinked and looked around as if I'd just woken him up. As he took in Daddy's armchair and Mama's rosebud wallpaper, I got the impression that he'd been very far away.

I touched his arm. "Are you all right?"

He considered that, then said, "All right." Shivering, he added, "Cold."

"I could get you a blanket, if you want. I think there's one in the linen closet."

"No," he said, rubbing his eyes. He motioned to the couch. "Sit down."

Obediently, I sat. I tried not to look at his sketchbook, but it was hard not to. Takuma wasn't doodling. He was actually drawing.

I grabbed the sketchbook. "You're an artist!"

Takuma took it back and swiftly turned the page, hiding whatever drawing he'd been working on. "Like Daniel," he whispered.

My heart ached. "Yes, like Daniel."

For a long time, we just sat there, staring at our hands. Mine itched to grab the sketchbook and paw through his new drawings, but I didn't want to rattle him. Besides, beating a sick man at a game of tug-of-war would have hardly been a challenge.

"You look?" he finally asked as he offered me the sketchbook.

I held my breath. "Is that okay?"

He half nodded, half shrugged.

Indecision froze my fingers, but before I could change my mind, he set the sketchbook in my lap. It was heavier than I'd expected, like it was carrying a heavy load. Suddenly, I didn't want to look.

But Takuma was insistent, so reluctantly, I opened it. He'd been drawing feverishly for days, but the first couple of pages still belonged to my brother. There was the close-up of the soldier we'd never had a chance to meet, and there was the wide shot of the valley where he'd ultimately died. The charcoal had smudged over time, but the smudging looked deliberate, like these sketches were supposed to look fuzzy, incomplete.

I hurried through the rest of Daniel's drawings, ignoring the dull ache in my chest. Daniel was dead and buried, but Takuma was still here. When I reached one of a courtyard, I stopped flipping the pages. The lines were sharper, more distinct, and I didn't recognize the rows of soldiers. Their uniforms were lighter, and their helmets were oddly shaped.

Takuma tapped the drawing. "I guard emperor."

I squinted at the soldiers. "You were one of those little guys?"

I tried to picture him in a funny-looking helmet, but the image wouldn't settle. It was hard to picture him fighting in a war on either side.

Tentatively, I turned the page, revealing a length of beach

and a funny-looking hill. It looked vaguely familiar, but my brain was probably playing tricks on me.

"Ee-oh-toe," he said.

"What's ee-oh-toe?" I asked.

Takuma tapped the drawing.

"Oh," was all I said as I felt my cheeks get hot.

Ee-oh-toe was probably the name of the island. That wasn't so scary. Still, I held my breath as I turned the page. I wasn't sure what I was waiting for, but I was waiting for something.

The next sketch was of a box partly buried in the dirt. It only looked big enough to hold one soldier, maybe two.

"I make," Takuma said as he stuck out his chest.

"You *made* that box?" I asked. It explained why he was good at building towers out of dishes.

"I make *many*," he replied.

I wrinkled my nose. "What were they for?" They didn't look like they would fit even a single cot.

Takuma's chest deflated. "Kill boxes," he mumbled.

I swallowed, hard. Had Takuma killed my cousin in a box like that?

My insides turned to jelly as that awful thought sank in, and it was all that I could do not to shove the sketchbook off my lap. But before I had a chance to give it back to him, Takuma turned the page, revealing what I assumed was the same beach. We were on the hill this time, with the whole island spread before us. The ocean was rough and choppy—and dotted with dozens of ships.

"They come," Takuma said.

My hands started to tingle. I didn't want to see the rest. I didn't want to know. Takuma must have sensed my hesitation, because he didn't turn the page. Gratefully, I let it go. When it tumbled down my legs, I didn't even try to stop it.

A few of the pages turned themselves as the sketchbook gathered speed. By the time it hit the floor, Takuma's final drawing—the one that he'd been working on when I bumped his hand—was staring up at us. It was a close-up of a man, not Japanese, who looked like he was shouting. The gash I'd made Takuma draw had turned into a rifle.

With slightly quaking hands, I picked the sketchbook up. My eyes started at the barrel, then moved up the hand, the arm. Hatred boiled in my stomach—that arm, that hand, that gun had to belong to the man who'd killed him—but when I reached the face, I froze.

The face belonged to Robby.

A sob caught in my throat and came out as a gasp. My gaze darted back and forth between Robby and the rifle. I barely recognized the angry man shouting at Takuma. He looked nothing like the Robby in Auntie Mildred's photographs.

The sketchbook started to tremble. That must have meant my hands were trembling, too. When Takuma tried to take it, I didn't bother to object.

"Ella Mae?" he whispered.

Ee-oh-toe was Iwo Jima. Ee-oh-toe was where my cousin had murdered my best friend.

I dragged a hand under my nose. I had to get away. Being

around Takuma hadn't made me feel uncomfortable since that very first day, but now I couldn't sit beside him without bouncing in my seat. My flesh and blood had killed him. He must have thoroughly despised us.

"I'm sorry," I said as I bolted for the stairs. "I'm sorry, sorry, sorry."

Takuma called my name, but I didn't stop, didn't slow down. With his leg the way it was, he wouldn't be able to come after me. When I reached my room, I slammed the door shut on my heels and threw myself onto my bed. I tried to lose myself in the squiggles on the ceiling, but this awful, creeping guilt was too heavy to ignore. The only thing that I could think about was how it would feel to kill someone. And how it would feel to die.

25

A few minutes or a few hours later, Mama tromped upstairs. "I saw Takuma's pictures."

I scrubbed the tears out of my eyes. "They're not pictures, they're drawings." That was what Daniel had always said.

Mama didn't seem concerned about what they were or weren't. "He said they made you sad."

A drop of guilt leaked out of me. Of course he'd make me sound less crazy than I actually was.

"This doesn't change anything," she said.

"No, it changes *everything.*"

Mama sat down on the bed. The mattress groaned beneath her weight. "No one has to know the truth." When she realized what she'd just said, she sighed. "No one but you and me."

I didn't think that I could carry so much truth around.

She patted my knee. "I know it seems like this will never be okay again, but you know how these things are."

I plopped my chin into my hands. "I don't see how this will *ever* find a way of working itself out."

"Oh, don't be sensational. That's your auntie's job."

"But Robby shot him, Mama. Robby *killed* Takuma. Doesn't that erase all the good things that we've done?"

"Well, for one thing, *we* didn't shoot him." She tucked one of my braids behind my ear. "And for another, even if we had, why couldn't we ask for forgiveness?"

I might have acted like a scalawag, but the truth was, I'd never asked for anyone's forgiveness before. I'd thought that me and Mama were scoring points in heaven for taking Takuma in and standing up for him—and that those points made us better than the other folks we knew. But it hadn't occurred to me that maybe I'd thought we were better than Takuma, too. That I was doing him a favor by being his friend.

How had I never realized that Takuma was the one who was doing *me* the favor?

Mama bumped me with her shoulder. "Just go down there and talk to him."

I didn't move a muscle. I didn't want to talk. If we talked, then I would have to put these feelings into words, and I doubted I could do that even if I'd wanted to.

Mama clucked her tongue. "Of course, if you'd rather do some housework, I'm sure that I could find a toilet for you to clean."

Reluctantly, I stood back up and headed toward the stairs.

"Oh, and Ella Mae?" Mama said.

Slowly, I turned back around.

"Just remember that you owe this friendship to whatever happened." She folded her arms across her waist. "Sometimes a little good can grow out of a lot of bad."

I found Takuma sitting on Mama's swing in the backyard. His head was tipped back, and his eyes were closed. He didn't have his sketchbook, though he still had a pencil tucked behind his ear. Guess there wasn't much to draw once you'd recorded your whole life and death.

I scuffed my foot. "Do you want to go for a walk?" I'd always thought talking was easier when I was walking, too.

Takuma thumped his leg. It looked as stiff as an old board. "No walk today," he said.

I probably should have guessed that. "So what do you want to do?"

"May-so?" he asked.

"May what?"

Takuma shook his head. "No mind."

I dug my toe into the crack between two bricks in the patio. Daniel and Daddy had laid it back when I was two or three, so even though they'd let me help, I'd mostly gotten in the way. When I dropped a brick on my finger, Daddy had just rolled his eyes, but Daniel had scooped me up and carried me inside the house. I never found out where they'd laid my brick, but secretly, I hoped that it was one of these, that it was tying Daniel to Takuma and me to both of them.

"I'm sorry," I said again. "I wish I could say or do *something,* but I just—"

"Ella Mae," he interrupted. He waited until I met his gaze. "No sorry. Never sorry."

My eyes watered like a leaky faucet. I must have developed allergies in the last couple of days. It was the only explanation.

"Do you want to talk about it?" I asked.

Takuma shook his head, but slowly, like he could tell I didn't want to.

"It's okay," I said after drawing a deep breath. "I want you to tell me. Really. It's about time I started acting like the friend I claim to be."

He smiled, a little. "I make boxes," he said slowly. "Holes in mountain, too."

I scrunched up my nose. "How'd you make holes in a mountain?"

He made a stick out of his hands, then pretended to throw it across the grass. When it hit, he covered his ears.

"Dynamite!" I said. "You made caves with dynamite!"

"Dynamite," Takuma said, trying out the new word.

I nodded reassuringly. "So what were the caves—the holes in mountains—for?"

"For live," Takuma said, then added softly, "and for die."

I shuddered despite the warm spring breeze. Why had Takuma died when so many others lived? Of course, maybe if he hadn't, the Allies would have lost the war. I didn't like that idea, but I didn't like the idea of Takuma lying in the dirt, either. The trade-offs weren't cut-and-dried when you cared about people on both sides.

"We wait long time," he went on. "Hole in mountain shake."

"Why didn't you fight back?" I asked. I didn't like the thought of Takuma fighting—killing—but I didn't like the thought of him just sitting there, either.

Takuma shrugged. "No hope. Kuribayashi say we die, so we wait. We wait and hide."

"Caw-coo-say," I mumbled. It was the first Japanese word he'd taught me. I hadn't liked it then, and I certainly didn't like it now.

"Yes, caw-coo-say," he said. "Like Theo."

I wished his game of hide-and-seek had turned out as well as Theo's.

"They reach top of mountain," he went on. "Then they rise flag."

I perked up. "They raised a flag in the middle of the battle?" It must have been the first raising. I knotted my arms across my chest. "I probably should have known."

Most folks didn't realize that there had been two raisings: the first when they reached the top of the island's highest point and the second, hours later, when there was a reporter present. By the end of the battle, most of the boys who'd launched that first attack were lying in a row of bodies, waiting to be shipped home to their families. And no one even remembered the first flag that they'd raised.

No one except Takuma.

"Nakamura yell. They shoot." Takuma dropped his gaze. "We watch Nakamura die."

I swallowed, hard. "Is that when . . . ?" I couldn't bring myself to ask, *Is that when Robby shot you?*

Takuma shook his head. "No, Miyazaki next. He run after Nakamura. They were friends—no, brothers."

I thought I understood what he was trying to say. Nakamura loved Miyazaki in the same way I loved him.

"Then," he went on, but before he could get the words out, he started to cough. He coughed for what felt like forever, but just when I decided it was time to go for Mama, he cleared his throat and tried again: "They shoot fire," he croaked.

I'd seen the old newsreels, so I'd seen flamethrowers in action. Or at least I'd seen them take out a bunch of lifeless dummies. It was harder to imagine them shooting actual people, especially people who were huddled at the back of a man-made cave, waiting patiently for death. What had they thought about as they'd waited there to die? Had it ever occurred to them that some cockamamie scientist might bring them back to life?

"I run," Takuma said. His breath was coming in short spurts, but whether that was because of the coughing or the memory, I couldn't decide. "But fire everywhere. I fall. And when I look up, he . . ."

Takuma didn't have to say who *he* was. Guilt twisted my insides, but I tried to ignore it.

"He rise rifle. I rise hands. Then everything go white."

I squeezed my eyes shut—I didn't want to see Takuma's hands (or Robby's rifle, for that matter)—but my eyelids made a better screen than the backyard ever could have. Before I could tell it not to, my brain replayed the scene as Takuma had described it. I could almost taste the fire, smell the burned meat in the air. My eyes opened on their own.

I must have made a face, because Takuma's forehead crinkled. "Ella Mae?" he asked softly.

"I'm fine," I said through gritted teeth.

"No," he said, "not fine."

I half laughed, half sobbed. It was the same thing I'd told him when his leg gave out.

Takuma smiled softly, and fresh tears sprang to my eyes. For once, I let them fall. I was tired of lying to myself. It was time to stop pretending I was something that I wasn't.

"Do you forgive me?" I peeped, drying my cheeks off on my sleeve. "For thinking I was better?"

He thought about that for a moment, then dragged himself out of the swing. "I give my forgive," he said. He could barely stand up straight, but he bowed, anyway. "*Always* give my forgive."

I felt my face flush. Things felt strange between us, but they felt better, too. I'd never thought of us as equals. It was about time.

"I hear your birthday's comin' up," I said. "Want to help me plan a party?"

26

After a lengthy debate, we decided to have the party in our backyard. I'd wanted to have it on the platform out back, but Mama had informed us that she'd given up tree-climbing after giving birth to Daniel, and since she was the one who'd be providing the refreshments, she wanted someplace more accessible. When Takuma suggested the backyard as a compromise, we'd both taken the deal.

Once we agreed on a location, we turned our attention to the guest and shopping lists. The shopping list was easy. Takuma ate pork links like most folks ate potato chips, and I thought orange juice went really well with ground-up pig. Mama thought that we should serve these things called petit fours, but I refused to eat something that I couldn't pronounce. When Takuma suggested waffles, we compromised again.

The guest list was trickier. We couldn't invite the Clausens, and without Gracie as a lure, Chester definitely wouldn't come. The Lloyds and the Leavitts were obviously out, and Mr. Jaeger wasn't really the world's best party guest. That left the Dents, the Whitmans, and Miss Shepherd, but given our track record, I wasn't of a mind to ask.

Mama let us agonize for the rest of the night and into the next morning, but before I left for school, she took away our shopping list and tucked it into her purse. There wasn't going to be any party if we didn't get our supplies, so as soon as I got home, she dragged us to the store.

I watched Takuma in the side mirror as we jounced up Radley Way. He was leaning on the window, forehead pressed against the glass, and every time we hit a pothole, he closed his eyes and winced.

"Are you all right?" I whispered. He didn't look all right to me, but telling folks what we really thought wasn't supposed to be courteous. Why didn't we make more of an effort to be honest? It probably would have saved us a lot of grief down the road.

Takuma straightened up—he must have realized I was watching—then forced a tired smile. "Yes, ma'am," he said, but as soon as he thought I wasn't looking, he sagged back against the window.

I wasn't convinced, but I didn't press him, either. Who was I to tell him what he could and couldn't lie about?

By the time we reached the store, Takuma looked as white as Auntie Mildred's gloves. I raised my eyebrows as he climbed out of the car, but he didn't dissolve into tears, just nodded resolutely.

"You don't have to pretend," I said. "It's all right if you're hurt . . ."

I trailed off when I realized that neither he nor Mama was listening to me. They were both gawking at another car, their eyes as wide as flying saucers. I glanced over my shoulder to see what they were looking at.

It was the Clausens' Chrysler.

Mama was the first to pick her chin up off the ground. "You won't say a word," she hissed as she took hold of my hand. "Not one word, you understand? I don't care if your auntie punches you in the nose. You will not say one word."

I didn't want to say *a* word; I wanted to say several dozen. I wanted to race into the store and corner her around the Brillo Pads. She'd have no choice but to listen, and I'd have no choice but to tell her that this was Robby's fault. That he'd murdered Takuma.

Mama squeezed my hand. "I said, do you understand?"

I resisted for a moment, then gritted my teeth and said, "Yes, ma'am." Under my breath, I added, "Wouldn't want to knock over Mr. Whitman's Brillo Pads."

First, we headed for the pork links, where I loaded up the cart with enough prepackaged sausages to keep St. Jude fed for months. Mama didn't help, but that was just as well. She'd never been a fan of prepackaged anything.

Next, we headed for dry goods. We would have headed faster if it hadn't been for Takuma, who was leaning on the cart like an old man on his cane. His breath was coming in wet pants, as if his lungs were full of liquid, and every time he coughed, the cart rattled like a bag of bones. If it hadn't been half-full of pork links, I would have picked him up and stuck him in the cart, too.

In dry goods, we grabbed a bag of flour and a jar of cardamom (which was Mama's secret ingredient for making melt-in-your-mouth waffles). Just before we turned the corner, a flash of blond hair caught my eye. I only caught a glimpse, but it was Gracie, no doubt about it. I'd know that blond hair anywhere.

Mama must have seen her, too, because she pressed her lips into a line. But instead of abandoning our cart, she said, "There's no sense turnin' back."

In produce, I scooped up every orange that Mr. Whitman had (since frozen orange juice was for soldiers and folks who didn't have my impressive arm muscles). I placed them in the cart one orange at a time, careful not to set them where they might roll out.

If Mama noticed the amount of food we were about to purchase, she didn't mention it, just led us toward the check stand. Takuma plodded after her, pushing the cart ahead of him. I kept an eye out for Auntie Mildred, sweeping one way, then the other, just like Sergeant Friday. That woman was a wily one.

But by the time we reached the check stands, she was still nowhere to be found, and I started to relax. The last few weeks had made me paranoid. She wasn't really going to confront us in front of God and everyone. I stuck our groceries on the conveyor belt while Mama sagged against the Clark Bars. Takuma leaned against the cart. When he coughed, it bumped her leg.

At least that got her attention. Mama frowned at the conveyor belt. "Do we really need so many pork links?"

I blew a string of hair out of my face as I grappled with the flour. "The last thing you want to do is run out of refreshments." I decided not to mention that I'd learned that from Auntie Mildred.

Mama didn't have a chance to answer before Patrick Temple turned his phony grin on us. He was a year older than Gracie, but his cowlick made him seem younger. When his eyes flicked to Takuma, his phony grin faltered, but at least he didn't sneer.

"Good afternoon!" he said brightly. It sounded like he'd just sucked the air out of a helium balloon. "Did you find what you were looking for?"

"Looks like they found more than that," a familiar voice said.

27

I didn't turn around at first. I didn't want to draw Auntie Mildred's attention. Mama would take care of this. That was what mamas were for.

"This is none of your beeswax," Mama said, "so you might as well just leave us be."

Auntie Mildred sneered. "Oh, it's my beeswax," she said. "When you let that *thing* attack my daughter—"

"He didn't attack me," Gracie said, coming up behind her mama. "The truth is, I kissed *him.*"

Auntie Mildred's nostrils flared, but she didn't box Gracie's ears, just inched closer to Mama. "That's some nerve you have, bringing that thing out in public. I have half a mind to drag it to the pound!"

I had to clench my teeth to keep from biting her myself.

Mama held her hands up. "You don't know what you're sayin', so if you'd stop makin' a scene—"

"You think I'm the one makin' a scene?" Auntie Mildred waved at Patrick (who was studiously inspecting a hangnail), then at Mr. Whitman's other customers (who were creeping closer to our check stand when they thought no one was looking). "*You're* the one subjectin' them to that unnatural Jap!"

She would have gotten less attention if she'd fired off a flare. The other customers stopped creeping and simply gawked outright. Theo, who'd been loitering around the frozen foods, turned tail and tried to flee, but before he could escape, the crowd shifted, hemming him in.

"Don't do that," Mama said. "Don't try to place the blame on me. It ain't anyone's fault, you understand?" She grabbed Auntie Mildred's elbow and said those words again: "It ain't anyone's fault."

Gracie grabbed her other elbow. "He isn't what you think he is. He's a kind, sweet, gentle boy who—"

"He is no such thing!" Auntie Mildred sputtered as she said it, so she had to wipe her chin off with her sleeve. "And you're a fool for thinkin' otherwise."

Gracie had to wipe her chin off, too, as she yanked her mama's elbow. "I think we'd better go."

"I'll go when I feel like goin', and I don't feel like goin' yet." Auntie Mildred ripped her elbow out of Gracie's grip. "I know what you're doin', Anna. You think you're gonna pin this mess on me. All right, then, I admit it. I tried to bring Robby back to life." She stuck her chin out at Takuma. "But I didn't decide to keep that miserable *thing*."

For a second, maybe more, it was so still that I could hear the fluorescent lights buzzing overhead. The other customers just stood there gaping in various states of disbelief. Mrs. Leavitt's nose crinkled, and Chester's eyes and mouth widened into three perfect Os. Theo looked like the only one who wasn't in shock, but the crowd had gone so rigid that he couldn't escape.

I tried to take a step toward the door, but my feet wouldn't budge. Was I in shock, too? I'd never thought that Auntie Mildred would make such a fuss in public.

When Mama cleared her throat, I expected her to tell the whole world what we knew. But instead of coming clean, she set her sights on Patrick. "How much do I owe you?"

Patrick glanced at the register. "Eight dollars," he said, then glanced at it again. "Well, eight dollars and nine cents."

"Very well," Mama said as she retrieved her wallet.

Auntie Mildred made a face. "Are you really gonna pay your bill and walk away from me?"

"Thank you, Patrick," Mama said as she handed him the money. I couldn't help but notice that her hands were trembling slightly. "I'm sorry for the scene." As she returned her wallet to her purse, she added, "Yes, Mildred, I am."

Mama turned to go, but Auntie Mildred grabbed her wrist.

"Don't you turn your back on me!" she said as she whipped Mama around.

Mama's elbow bumped the Clark Bars, knocking a few onto the ground. She glanced down at the candy, then back up at her sister, her gaze as piercing as a tiger's. "You will take your hands off me this instant, or I will take them off for—"

She didn't have a chance to finish before Auntie Mildred

slapped her. It happened so fast that I couldn't process what I'd seen until the red spot bloomed on Mama's cheek.

Red-hot rage gripped my heart and made my shoulders quake, but before I had a chance to do much more than shake, Mr. Whitman appeared out of nowhere. The rotten tomatoes on his apron glistened like fresh blood.

"I'm sorry," he said, "but I'm afraid I have to ask you two to take this fight outside."

For once, I didn't argue, just grabbed Takuma's hand and dragged him toward the door. The only way out was around Patrick, who also appeared to be inching toward the exit sign. Mama, on the other hand, hadn't moved a muscle, probably because her sister was still gripping her wrist.

I glanced over my shoulder. "Gracie, get your mama!"

"I'm trying!" Gracie said.

I knew how I'd make her budge—it involved a swift kick in the fanny—but I couldn't abandon Takuma. He could barely stand up straight, and it didn't strike me as a good idea to leave him in the middle of what could easily become a brawl. Chester was weaving toward us, apparently coming to our aid, but before he could find an opening, the crowd shifted again. Guess we were on our own.

We were halfway to the door when Auntie Mildred started wailing. It made me think of how she'd howled like a coyote at the lab, but instead of clawing at a window, she clawed at Mama's arm. Gracie tried to intervene, but she only succeeded in knocking them off balance. When Auntie Mildred hit the ground, I thought that might be the end of it, but when she clambered to her knees, she was still going strong.

"—gonna get rid of him," she was saying, "or so help me, I'll disown you!" At some point in the scuffle, her hat had fallen off. Now it was dangling from her hair like a dead bug from a web, but she didn't seem to notice. "I won't speak to you at parties, I won't invite you to my own, and it'll be like you're dead to—"

"Robby killed him!" Mama screamed. "He was lyin' on the ground, and Robby shot him in cold blood."

It took me a few seconds to realize what she'd just said, but when it registered, I froze. No one dared to move or even breathe. Even Mr. Lloyd had the good sense not to scoff. The silence was so perfect that I could hear the blood gushing through my ears. Robby had once pressed a seashell to my ear and told me it was the ocean, but even then, I'd known the truth. That gushing sound was blood, the sound of life and everything.

Auntie Mildred sat back on her heels. "You lie," she mumbled dully, but no one seemed to believe her. I doubted she believed herself.

"He drew a picture," Mama whispered. "Robby's face was plain as day, and he had both hands on the gun."

Auntie Mildred swatted at those words like they were pesky flies. "No, that can't—you must have shown him—"

"I didn't show him anything," Mama interrupted. "But it's Robby, no doubt about it."

Auntie Mildred slumped against a rack of the *Ladies' Home Journal.* "I don't—I mean, I can't—"

"You can," Mama replied, wrapping an arm around her shoulders. For some reason, they looked even thinner than usual. "You don't have a choice."

Auntie Mildred didn't answer, just kept swatting at those words like she thought that they might sting. The crowd shifted uneasily, but before they could wander off, Takuma made a move.

He could barely stand up straight, but that didn't prevent him from hobbling around the Clark Bars. He had to hold on to the check stand to keep from falling over, but when he stopped in front of Auntie Mildred, he held out his hand.

For a long time, she just gaped at him. Her expression flickered back and forth between remorse and revulsion, and I swallowed, hard. I didn't trust Auntie Mildred to make the right decision, but she was the only one who could. Finally, she drew a shaky breath and placed her hand in his.

The crowd gasped in surprise—I probably gasped, too—but Takuma only grunted as he dragged her to her feet. Their toes brushed as they struggled to regain their balance, but Auntie Mildred didn't shudder, didn't even pull away.

"Sorry Robby," he whispered.

She let out a sob, then pressed her face into her hands.

Takuma didn't wait for Auntie Mildred to stop crying, just sagged against the check stand, obviously out of breath. I was still too stunned to react, but Mama sidled up to him and offered herself as a crutch. He draped an arm around her shoulders, and she slid one around his waist, and then they half staggered, half skidded through the sea of Clark Bars and around a speechless Patrick. As I watched them lumber off, leaning on each other like the two sides of an arch, my heart glowed so fiercely that I thought it might burst.

28

Mama thought we should wait to bake Takuma's cake, but I wanted to make it as soon as we got home. For some reason, it felt like we were running out of time. Takuma seemed all right while me and Mama mixed the batter and stuck the cake pans in the oven, but he started to cough as soon as the timer buzzed. By the time we got the cake pans to the cooling racks we'd spread out on the table, Takuma was on his hands and knees, a thin line of drool and snot dangling out of his mouth.

"It's all right," Mama said, handing him a clean dishrag. "Let's get you into a chair."

It didn't look all right to me, but mamas knew best. She looped one of his arms around her neck, and I looped the other around mine. When we set him down in Daniel's chair, it didn't even groan.

Though she might have sounded calm, Mama looked like a whirlwind as she swept around the kitchen. I tried not to bounce as she filled a pot with water and stuck it on a burner, then hacked up her biggest lemon and a chunk of ginger root. She was already going as fast as she could.

Daddy must have wondered why she was hacking up ginger root, because he turned up in the archway as she dumped it in the pot. "What are you making now?" he asked.

"What does it look like?" I replied. Honestly, he asked the dumbest questions.

Daddy managed to ignore me. "Anna, what's going on?"

"He just has a cough," she said as she stirred the lemon tea.

Daddy cocked an eyebrow. "That doesn't sound like just a cough to me."

"Well, you'd be more than welcome to go and get a flask of brandy."

"Aren't you making lemon tea?"

"Only because we're out of spirits."

Daddy threw his arms up. "You said it was just a cough!"

"And *you* said it didn't sound like just a cough to you."

He folded his arms across his chest. "Well, I trust your diagnosis." Under his breath, he added, "I'm not wasting brandy on a cold."

I stuck both hands on my hips. "I think you meant to say you're not wastin' brandy on a Jap."

Mama threw her hot pads down. "Watch your language, Ella Mae!"

But she didn't have a chance to locate her bar of Ivory before Takuma coughed again. He covered his mouth like a good boy, but when he pulled the dishrag back, it was covered with red spots. He'd sprayed the cake pans, too.

I pressed my lips into a line. Throwing up was one thing, but coughing blood was another.

Mama gawked at the dishrag, then blinked and shook her head. "Clean that up," she told me in her no-nonsense voice. "And *don't* forget to wash your hands as soon as you're finished."

"Are you happy now?" I asked as I scowled up at Daddy.

Instead of answering, he licked his lips. At least he didn't *look* happy.

Mama cleared her throat. "The brandy, Jed?" she pressed.

"Yes, of course," he mumbled, then bumped into the doorjamb in his haste to get away. The coatrack rattled in the entryway as he retrieved his hat and coat, and then the door slammed shut behind him.

When Mama scurried up the stairs, it was just me and Takuma. I scrubbed his dishrag out with soap and water, then turned my attention to the cake. I took a close look at both layers, turning them this way and that, but in the end, I decided it wasn't worth the risk. The fact that he'd coughed blood obviously had everyone spooked, so with a heavy heart, I chucked both cakes in the trash.

"Sorry," he said, cringing.

"It ain't your fault," I replied as I attacked the table with another dishrag. "You can't help bein' sick."

"Not sick," Takuma whispered.

A shiver skittered down my spine, but I pretended not to notice. "Don't be ridiculous," I said. "You'll feel better in the morning."

"Ella Mae," he said, then waited until I met his gaze. His eyes were red but clear. "*Not* sick."

It sounded like he meant it, but I didn't want him to be right, and besides, how did he know? Daddy was going to get the brandy, and he was going to be fine. But I didn't have a chance to tell him before Mama reappeared.

She motioned toward the dishrag I'd been using to clean up. "Throw that away," she said, then changed her mind at the last second. "No, I guess I'll take it. We should probably burn it."

Mama only burned things she really wanted to get rid of. Either that dishrag had offended her, or it was dangerous to keep around. I tried not to think too hard about which it was as I plopped it into her hand.

"Now go upstairs and wash your hands. Make sure you use the lye. And *don't* forget to scrub all the way up to your elbows!"

She hadn't even finished before I spun around. Mama's sudden obsession with proper hygiene was starting to scare me. I dug the lye out of the cupboard and rubbed it under the faucet to work up a good lather, then scrubbed my hands and arms until they practically bled. I thought that I was trying to wash Takuma's blood away, but as I watched the suds rinse down the drain, I realized that I was really trying to wash the memory away, too. *Not sick,* he'd said so certainly. I wished I couldn't remember.

That night, I waited for sleep, but it never bothered to show up. I tried to welcome it by climbing into bed as soon as I finished my dinner, but I could hear Takuma coughing, so it was hard to fall asleep. He sounded like the old man who sat outside Arty's Tavern smoking cigarettes all day. But Takuma hadn't smoked a single cigarette in his whole life—or his whole *second* life, at least.

Hours after sunset, Mama and Daddy trudged upstairs. They were speaking softly, but if I concentrated, I could turn their whispers into words.

"—can't go on like this," Daddy was saying. He sounded downright weary.

Mama laughed, not very nicely. "Well, it's not like we can quit." She just sounded mad.

"He needs a doctor," Daddy said.

"Well, you and me both know that Dr. Olsen won't treat him."

"Can you blame him?" Daddy asked. "He lost two sons in the Pacific."

"And I lost Daniel in the Ardennes. Does that mean I get to hate every German in the world?"

"I don't know," he whispered. "Maybe."

Mama just harrumphed.

"At least let me call that scientist. What was his name again?"

"You will *not* call Dr. Franks! He would only kill him faster."

I sat straight up in bed. Had I heard Mama right? Was Takuma really dying?

"Well, what are we supposed to do, just sit and watch him waste away?"

"We're supposed to keep him comfortable," Mama said, then sighed. "But beyond that, I don't know."

I strained to catch Daddy's response, but their door clicked shut behind them before he whispered it. I waited for breathless minutes, hoping against hope that they'd come back, but they must have gone to bed. Reluctantly, I lay back down.

I rolled onto my stomach and pressed my face into my pillow, but it wasn't any use. If I'd been wide awake before, I was wider awake now. What if Mama had it right? What if it really was Takuma's last night on this earth? I didn't want to waste it sleeping. I pressed my hand against the wall and tried to pass my strength to him.

29

When I woke up the next morning, it felt like I'd forgotten something. I scrubbed the sleep out of my eyes and took a look around. The light slanting through the curtains was coming from the east, so it couldn't have been later than six (or maybe seven).

I flopped back on the mattress and tried to remember. As I stared up at the squiggles, the events of the previous day came rushing back. I scrambled out of bed and headed for Takuma's room, but when the doorbell dinged, I headed for the stairs instead. I didn't know who was at the door, but if he woke Takuma up, I might have to kick him in the shins.

I stumbled down the stairs and yanked open the door. At the sight of Dr. Franks, I froze. He wasn't wearing his lab coat, but his mustache was unmistakable.

"What are you doin' here?" I asked.

"Your father called," Dr. Franks said. For once, he wouldn't meet my gaze. "He said the subject's been—"

"Stay back!" I interrupted, brandishing an umbrella like a broadsword.

Dr. Franks held up his hands. "I apologize for the intrusion, but your father was insistent."

Daddy came up behind me as if he'd just been summoned. "You must be Dr. Franks."

Dr. Franks held out his hand. "And you must be Mr. Higbee."

Daddy shook the offered hand. "You can call me Jed," he said as he pulled the door open. I tried to push it closed, but Daddy was a lot stronger than I was.

If Dr. Franks noticed our tug-of-war, he didn't mention it. "Thank you," was all he said as he stepped into the entryway.

Mrs. Timothy said that the elements would combine against the Devil, so I waited for the walls to cave (or at least tremble a little), but the old house only sighed. It looked like the combining was going to be up to me.

"Mama doesn't want you here," I said, folding my arms across my chest. "And neither do I."

Daddy picked me up and set me off to the side. "Would you like some coffee?" he asked Dr. Franks. "Or perhaps some lemon tea?"

Dr. Franks waved that away. "Oh, no, that's all right. I'm perfectly hydrated." He removed his hat and coat (which looked like it could swallow children whole). "I just want to see the subject."

"We've been over this," I said. "It's Takuma, not 'the subject.'"

Daddy didn't comment, just took the hat and coat. "This way," he replied as he handed them to me.

I crinkled my nose. "I don't want to touch his things."

Daddy waved that off. "Just hang them up," he mumbled. "Then feel free to come upstairs."

Grudgingly, I took the hat and coat. At least Daddy wasn't trying to cut me out of the deal. But as soon as they turned their backs, I chucked his things at the coatrack. The hat missed it completely, but the coat managed to land on one of the pegs.

Dr. Franks raced up the stairs. "I jumped in my car as soon as I received your message. When exactly did the coughing start?"

Before Daddy could reply, Mama materialized at the top of the stairs. Her robe was limp and rumpled (though it wasn't even seven thirty), but she looked more than capable of dealing with Dr. Franks.

"Out!" she said indignantly. Her shoulders shook with rage.

"Mrs. Higbee," he replied, "please allow me to explain."

"There's nothing to explain," she said as she herded him back down.

Dr. Franks clung to the railing. "You don't understand," he said as he struggled to hang on. "The last thing I want to do is watch the sub—I mean, Takuma—die."

Mama missed a step. Dr. Franks had clearly said what she'd wanted to hear. He must have noticed, too, because he hurried on.

"We're in a race here—a real race—to unlock the secrets of life. While other scientists have tinkered with their silly children's toys, we've asked the daunting questions and followed lines of research that would have made lesser men blanch. And Takuma is the key." He drew a ragged breath. "I want to save him, Mrs. Higbee, maybe even more than you do. Please do me the favor of allowing me to try."

As he caught his breath, the teeter-totter seemed to shift. Mama grabbed the railing as she rocked back on her heels, obviously overcome by the power of his words. Daddy tried to help her, but she knocked his hand away.

Dr. Franks knotted his hands as if in prayer. "*Please*," he said again. "I've never begged for anything, but I'm begging you now. That is my life up there."

Even I had to admit that it was a moving speech. Takuma felt like my life, too.

But Mama didn't yield, just pressed her lips into a line. Finally, she turned to me. "What do you think, Ella Mae?"

Her question took me by surprise. I wasn't used to making the decisions. I looked back and forth between them, searching for an answer to the riddle she'd presented, but if there was an answer (or even a riddle), I couldn't have said what it was. Finally, I peeped, "I think we should let him try."

Mama smoothed her robe. "Very well," she said as she glared at Dr. Franks. "But don't think for a second that this means we agree with you. We'll never agree, you understand?" When he nodded, Mama sighed. "But at least for the time being, we do want the same thing."

He tightened his grip on his black bag (which I hadn't

noticed until now). "Thank you, Mrs. Higbee." And with that, he bolted up the stairs.

While Mama and Daddy exchanged a heavy look, I hurried after him. The last thing *I* wanted to do was leave Dr. Franks alone with my best friend.

I might have only been a few seconds behind Dr. Franks, but when I reached Takuma's room, he was already unloading his black bag. If he'd noticed Daniel's drawings, they hadn't distracted him for long. While he unpacked his stethoscope, I crept closer to the bed. Takuma's skin was gray and papery, but his ruffled hair reminded me of Theo's on a windy day. He looked far too old for Gracie but far too young to die.

Dr. Franks motioned toward the nightstand. "Get that out of here," he said. He must have meant the broth that Mama had tried to feed Takuma.

Scowling, I retrieved the bowl—I wasn't Dr. Franks's nurse—but when I spied the broth, I frowned. It was flat and cold, untouched, which meant Takuma hadn't eaten since noon the day before. I didn't know much about keeping folks alive, but I was pretty sure they had to eat.

While I watched from Daniel's dresser, Dr. Franks took Takuma's pulse, then checked his heart and lungs. Takuma was so tired he didn't even lift his head. Next, Dr. Franks pulled out a flashlight and shined it in his eyes. I expected him to flinch, but he only lay there sleeping.

I set the bowl on Daniel's dresser. "How's he doin'?" I whispered, hugging my arms around my waist.

Dr. Franks ripped off his stethoscope. "Well, he's certainly not doing well. His motor neurons have completely failed. The cells themselves are dying now, tearing themselves apart. He likely won't survive the day if we don't take drastic action."

Mama appeared in the doorway. "What drastic action?" she replied.

Dr. Franks fiddled with his sleeve. "I've been developing another pod that will reshape existing cells in the same way the other grew them. The procedure *is* somewhat untested, but at this point, it's almost certainly the only chance he's got."

"But why is it untested?" Mama asked. "You said you could predict how his symptoms would progress. Doesn't that mean the other subjects have experienced the same things?"

Dr. Franks chuckled uneasily. "We only just finished construction—"

"Then try it out," Mama cut in, "and see how the procedure goes. If it works, we will consider bringing him in for a treatment. *If* he doesn't show any improvement on his own."

"You don't understand," he said.

"On the contrary," she said, "I understand completely. You've put all your faith in science, but we've put all our faith in God. So try your new procedure. See how it turns out. If it really works as well as you seem to think it will, then he'll probably be fine."

Dr. Franks lowered his gaze. "But that's just it," he mumbled. "We can't try the new procedure because we don't have anyone to try it on."

My breath caught in my throat. "What are you tryin' to say?"

Dr. Franks threw up his arms. "I'm saying he's the last man standing! The others have been dead for *weeks*." Sighing, he dropped his gaze. "Subject oh-one-eight is my last chance."

"Subject oh-one-eight," I murmured. "Was he really the eighteenth?"

Dr. Franks nodded.

I crinkled my nose. "But there were only eight or nine at that first demonstration."

There was something big, something important, that I was obviously missing. Thankfully, Mama figured it out.

"You *knew*," was all she said.

I didn't know what Dr. Franks was supposed to have known, but he didn't deny it.

"You've done this before," Mama went on, "so you knew what was gonna happen. You *knew* they were gonna die." She clenched her teeth. "But you still brought them back."

Though he had the decency to wince, Dr. Franks still didn't deny it.

"So Takuma must have seen what was happening to the others." I felt my shoulders droop. "He must have known that he was dying from the very first day."

Dr. Franks's nostrils flared. "No, he must have realized that he had a chance to *live*—for another month, another week. Wouldn't you give anything for another day of life?"

"But this wasn't his life," I replied. For the first time, I really understood that.

Dr. Franks stuck out his chin. "Evolution requires sacrifice."

I glanced down at Takuma, who looked like a worn-out paper doll. "Your sacrifice?" I asked. "Or his?"

Though Dr. Franks did blush, he didn't bother to reply, but that was just as well. Mama's face had flushed purple, and she looked like she might explode.

"Get out," she said through gritted teeth.

Dr. Franks's cheeks paled. "Excuse me?"

"You heard me," Mama said. *"Get out."*

Dr. Franks's eyes narrowed. "I don't think you appreciate the gravity of this situation. If you sit back and do nothing, subject oh-one-eight will die."

"His name is Takuma!" I replied at the same time Mama screamed, "GET OUT!"

At least that got his attention. After sneaking one last peek at Takuma, he refastened his black bag, then half sprinted, half lurched out the door and down the hall. Though it might have been sinful, I couldn't help but grin.

Daddy cleared his throat. I hadn't realized he'd come up-stairs. "Will you get his hat and coat?"

I thought about making a fuss, then immediately thought better of it. If it would get rid of him faster, I'd hold his coat for him myself. But by the time I got downstairs, he was already putting on his hat.

"I don't suppose you'd think about donating his remains," he said.

I folded my arms across my chest. "Who said there will be remains?"

My knees were almost knocking at the thought of losing my best friend, so this was less of a challenge than a bluff, and Dr. Franks called it.

"Oh, there will be remains." Dr. Franks glanced at his watch. "In fact, I'd say you're down to less than an hour now."

This announcement scared me more than I cared to admit, but I didn't want Dr. Franks to know that he'd gotten to me, so I just stuck out my tongue.

"I suppose I can take that as a no?" he asked.

"I suppose you can," I said.

"Then this concludes our business with each other." He stuck his hat back on his head. "I wish I could say it's been a pleasure."

"And I wish I could say we'd never met."

Dr. Franks didn't reply, just ripped open the door and stalked out of the house. It wasn't until his Cadillac was thundering away that I realized that wasn't true. I was very glad we'd met. If it hadn't been for Dr. Franks, I never would have known Takuma.

30

By the time I made it back upstairs, Takuma's eyes were open. They weren't sparkling anymore, but at least they smiled when they saw me. Mr. Higginbottom's mind had gone before he'd passed away, which must have been especially hard on the folks who'd cared about him most. At least when our eyes met, Takuma still smiled.

That made Mama turn around. When she spotted me, she smiled, too, and dragged herself out of the chair that she'd placed next to the bed. I couldn't decide whether the creaking was the chair or Mama's bones.

"He wants to see you," Mama said as she retrieved the bowl on Daniel's dresser.

I grabbed her hand. "You're not leavin'."

"Just for a minute," Mama said, cradling the bowl against her chest. The broth trembled like an upset pond every time she drew a breath. "I need to warm up some more broth and get another shot of brandy. The alcohol's been wearing off for the last couple of hours."

"Mama, wait," I said, tightening my grip on her hand. I

wasn't afraid of many things, but I was afraid of sitting in that chair, alone. Of watching Takuma die.

Mama seemed to understand. "You'll be all right," she whispered, easing her hand out of my grip. "I promise not to take too long."

I bit my lip and nodded bravely. If Takuma could stare death in the face, then maybe I could sit here with him while Mama warmed up some more broth.

As soon as Mama left, Takuma reached for me. "Ella Mae," he croaked.

I sat down in Mama's seat and took his outstretched hand. When he tried to tug me closer, I knelt down by the bed. The mattress dipped beneath my elbows as if they weighed more than Takuma and his patchwork quilt combined.

As I stared at our clasped hands, I noticed a smear of blood on his knuckles, but I didn't pull away. Yesterday, we'd been so careful about cleaning up his blood, but today, we knew the truth: whatever had come for Takuma had come for him alone.

"You knew what was happening," I whispered. "So why didn't you tell us?"

"Orange blossom fall," he said.

"What does that even mean?" I asked.

He opened his mouth to answer, but a cough came out instead. I handed him the washcloth Mama must have left behind, but he was too weak to pick it up, so I pressed it to his mouth for him. When he finally stopped coughing, I pulled the washcloth back. Fresh spots dotted the terry cloth, bright red on dingy white.

"Thank you," he replied, sinking back against his pillow.

I set the washcloth on the nightstand, more afraid of those red dots than I cared to admit. "Would you like a little broth? How about another shot of brandy? Mama said she'd be right back." I scrambled to my feet. "Maybe I should go and—"

"No!"

I choked back a sob as he fumbled for my hand. His grip was weaker than a kitten's, so I could have pulled away, but I let him pull me down instead. Love was holding someone's hand when you wanted to escape.

It only took a minute for my hand to start sweating. After another minute, I realized my knees were tingling, too. Still, I didn't try to move, just waited with Takuma. His eyes had closed again, and his mouth had fallen open. I watched his chest go up and down until, suddenly, it stopped.

I counted to ten, then peeped, "Takuma?"

He just lay there, dead or dying. It was hard to say for sure.

I squeezed his hand. "Takuma!"

Just before I screamed for Mama, Takuma squeezed mine back. As he drew a soggy breath, I collapsed onto the mattress.

"You can't do that," I said. "You can't leave me like that."

Takuma managed a weak grin. Only he would smile at a time like this.

"Mama was right," I mumbled, smashing my face into his quilt. "We should have sent you home when we still had the chance."

The grin melted off his face.

"You don't belong here," I went on as my eyes burned with unshed tears. "You're too good for us."

He rolled his tongue around his mouth. "You I belong," he croaked.

A single tear slipped down my cheek. "That's a real nice thing to say."

I expected him to fall asleep again, but he squeezed my hand instead. "Ella Mae—I want—"

He didn't have a chance to finish before he started coughing again. As I pressed the washcloth to his mouth, I wanted to scream or maybe cry, but I was too tired to do either, so I just sat there watching as he coughed his life away.

Finally, he drifted back into a tense half-sleep. I wiped off the red drool that had dripped onto his chin, then returned the washcloth to the nightstand. Since I couldn't do much for my hands, I just folded them in front of me.

"Pictures," he said, surprising me. I thought he'd fallen asleep. "I want—you have—pictures."

"All right," I said. "I'll keep 'em."

He nodded toward the walls. "Hang on?"

I knew what he meant, but what I said was, "I will if you will."

"Are-ee-got-toe," he said, grinning.

"Are-ee-got-toe," I replied, though I couldn't bring myself

to grin. Dying peacefully was one thing, but dying in pain was another. And he was going to die that way *twice*.

When Takuma drifted off again, I stared down at my hands, which were clasped as if in prayer. I wasn't saying one out loud, but according to Mrs. Timothy, Jesus could hear the silent prayers we whispered in our hearts. But if my heart was whispering anything, Jesus must not have heard it. The next time I glanced at Takuma, I realized that he'd stopped breathing.

This time, he didn't start again.

I leaned back instinctively, but he didn't try to grab me. My hands slid off the mattress and dangled at my sides. I stared at him until I couldn't stare another second, then took hold of the bedpost and hauled myself back to my feet.

Though I turned away from his still form, I couldn't bring myself to leave, so I clung to the bedpost and rehearsed the things I'd meant to tell him:

Your fingers look like Daniel's.

I choked on my first pork link.

I'm really sorry Robby shot you.

Then again, I'm really not.

Maybe that was what my heart had been whispering all along: *Please, God, tell Takuma all the things I never did.*

31

Mama came in not long after I hauled myself back to my feet. She smoothed the dents left by my elbows, then gently pulled the sheet over his head, ignoring the fresh tears that watered the flowers on her robe.

Daddy came in to retrieve me after she covered Takuma with the sheet. He led me from the room and silently steered me down the stairs. I'd lost all sense of time and place—it was like someone had turned my internal compass off—so I was glad that he was making all of these decisions for me.

In the kitchen, Daddy washed my hands (though he didn't scrub all the way up to my elbows), then planted me in Daniel's chair and pulled out Mama's pot. Oatmeal was the only thing that he knew how to make, but when he set the bowl in front of me, I just sat there staring. I was feeling lots of things, but hungry wasn't one of them.

"Come on," Daddy said as he nudged me with his foot. "You know you have to eat."

"I don't know anything," I mumbled as I fiddled with my spoon.

Daddy pursed his lips. "So you're just going to starve yourself to death?"

As soon as the words had left his mouth, he knew he'd made a mistake, but I didn't let him take them back.

"Don't see why not," I said. "If Takuma can, then so can I."

He sat down beside me. "Supergirl," he whispered. He hadn't called me that since I'd jumped off Uncle George's barn (and chipped my two front teeth). "He wouldn't want you to give up."

I jerked out of his reach. "How would you know what he wanted?"

Instead of answering, he blinked.

His ignorance just made me madder. "I know you hated him. I know you wished he'd never come. You probably thought he was abominable or some other such nonsense." I dug my fists into my eyes to disguise my angry tears. "But he was just my friend, nothing more and nothing less."

Daddy's Adam's apple bobbed. It looked like he was getting ready to rake me across the coals, but he just sank back in his seat and raked a hand through his dark hair. I lost track of the seconds that ticked off Mama's Kit-Cat clock before he cleared his throat.

"I didn't hate him," Daddy said. "But perhaps I did resent him."

I scrunched up my nose. "What is that supposed to mean?"

"It means I didn't understand him," Daddy said, then

sighed. "Or maybe I didn't understand why you risked so much for him."

I considered that for a long time. "I think we risked so much because we loved him."

"And that," Daddy replied, "is what I didn't understand."

I propped my elbows on the table. It was hard to say in words. "Haven't you ever cared about someone more than you cared about yourself?"

"Of course I have," he murmured. His voice was thick and scratchy. "I've loved you that much and more from the moment I laid eyes on you."

I lowered my gaze when I felt my cheeks get hot. It landed on the oatmeal, which was still letting off thin trails of steam. The raisins looked especially plump, and Daddy had added lots of sugar, just the way I liked it. Shyly, I retrieved the spoon.

"Thanks for the oatmeal," I mumbled, but what I really meant was, *I love you that much, too.*

Daddy must have understood, because he leaped back to his feet. When he started rinsing out the pot, I almost fell out of my chair. I'd never seen Daddy do the dishes before, but then, I'd never heard him say he loved me before, either. Mama said that death changed folks, but I never would have guessed that it could change them for the better.

After our awful morning, Mama didn't make me go to school, so I was flipping through the sketchbook when the doorbell dinged again. I returned it to its hiding place underneath the stairs, then went and got the door. I thought it might be Mr. Neeman, the man who ran the mortuary, but it was only Theo.

I folded my arms across my chest. "Aren't you supposed to be in school?"

Theo scuffed his foot. "I could ask you the same thing."

I unfolded my arms, since I was no longer interested in picking fights with Theo. "Mama said I didn't have to go."

"Funny, but mine said the same thing."

Instead of going our separate ways, me and Theo hemmed and hawed, drawing out our conversation. It felt nice to talk again. Finally, he produced a covered plate from behind his back.

"Anyway," he said, "she wanted me to give you these."

I recognized the gingersnaps as soon as I took the plate. "Auntie Mildred *baked*?" I asked. The bottom was still warm.

Theo looked down at his toes. "She got a bag of flour out as soon as we got home last night, and she's been bakin' ever since."

I looked down at mine, too. "Thanks, but Takuma passed away."

Theo's eyes bulged. "Takuma *what*?"

"I said, he passed away." Under my breath, I added, "Maybe you need to get your ears checked."

Theo rolled his eyes. "I heard what you—never mind. What I should have said is, 'I'm sorry.'" He flicked a curl out of his face. "I know how much he meant to you."

"Thanks," I mumbled glumly. Somehow, I'd never noticed how much effort it took to stay mad.

"You can keep the cookies," Theo said. "Gracie told us he likes gingersnaps."

"He does," I said, then swallowed. "Or at least he did."

Theo swallowed, too.

"Do you want to come in?" I asked as I pulled the door open. "I'm sure I could find us some milk."

Theo held his hands up. "Oh, no, that's all right." He sneaked a peek over my shoulder, as if he thought Takuma's ghost might appear at any minute. "Mama said I couldn't stay."

It was probably a lie (and not an especially good one), but I decided to let it go. "Tell Auntie Mildred I said thanks."

"I will," Theo replied as he hurried down the walk. "And I hope you like the cookies!"

"I'm sure we will," I said as my tears splattered the plastic wrap. Under my breath, I added, "And I'm sure he would have, too."

32

We had the funeral on Monday, at Neeman and Son Mortuary. Mr. Neeman and his son, the younger Mr. Neeman, were quiet, gangly men who smelled like vinegar and sweat, but they were kind men, too. They even cut us a deal on the embalming, since we weren't Takuma's next of kin. They said it was called the Good Samaritan's Discount.

We had the funeral in a room the Mr. Neemans called the chapel (though it was barely bigger than Mrs. Timothy's classroom). Of course, it didn't matter how big the chapel was or wasn't. Mr. Neeman and his son had the only thing I cared about, and that was the simple casket on the right side of the podium.

Mrs. Billings, who'd once attempted to turn me into a pianist, played the upright in the corner while I tried not to squirm. I'd submitted an obituary to the newspaper, but me and Mama didn't think that anyone was going to show. Still, Daddy had insisted that we not start until four. If this was going to be a proper funeral, then it was going to have a proper start.

When I checked the circle clock, it was only three minutes to four, so I propped my elbow on the armrest and wedged a fist under my chin. I was supposed to give a speech—Mama had called it the eulogy—and though I wasn't looking forward to getting up in front of everyone, I was looking forward to getting it over with.

Mrs. Billings had just finished the first verse of "God Is Love" when the outer door banged shut behind us. We turned around in unison just in time to see the Clausens materialize in the archway. I couldn't decide what I found more surprising—that they'd come at all or that they'd only shown up a minute early.

Auntie Mildred sighed. "Well, at least you haven't started."

Mama lurched out of her seat. "What are you doin' here, Mildred?"

"Same thing as you," she said, bumping Gracie into a pew. "But you'd better close that mouth if you want to keep it clear of flies."

Mama swallowed, hard. "I really don't know what to say."

"Then don't say anything," she said. "Now, for heaven's sake, can we sit down and just enjoy the service?"

Mama bit her lip—despite her previous statement, she must have wanted to say something—but instead of saying it, she obediently sat. She hardly ever did what Auntie Mildred told her to, so this was a small miracle in and of itself.

At precisely four o'clock, the younger Mr. Neeman rose, but before he had a chance to shuffle around the podium, the outer door banged shut again. When we turned around this time, Chester appeared in the archway, an off-white dishrag flung hastily over his shoulder.

"Sorry I'm late," he said to no one in particular. He yanked the dishrag off his shoulder and knotted it between his fists.

Auntie Mildred rolled her eyes. "You're not late, Mr. Richmond. Does it look like we've started?"

Chester turned as red as a maraschino cherry. He didn't bother to respond, just slipped silently into a pew. No sooner had he sat than Mr. Neeman stood back up, but he only made it halfway up the aisle before the door banged shut *again*.

Auntie Mildred whipped around. "Oh, for heaven's sake, this is a funeral, not *Ed Sullivan!*"

I just sat there smiling as Miss Shepherd, Arty Fletcher, and all four of the Dents shuffled sheepishly into the chapel. The Dents looked vaguely flustered (though that probably had more to do with the boy from the seesaw, who was steadily chewing through the ribbon on his sister's light blue dress), and I strongly suspected that Arty was skunk-drunk, but I was so happy that they'd come I almost kissed them on the cheeks.

As they spread out around the chapel, the younger Mr. Neeman took his place behind the podium. "Dear friends and—family," he said, tripping over that last word. He must have just remembered the Good Samaritan's Discount. "We're gathered here today in memory of . . ."

Instead of finishing that sentence, Mr. Neeman checked his notes. A part of me was mad that he'd forgotten, but

I pushed that part aside. It wouldn't have mattered to Takuma, so I tried not to let it matter to me, either.

I cleared my throat. "Takuma." I meant it to sound steady, but it came out as a croak.

Mr. Neeman didn't seem to notice. "We're gathered here today in memory of Takuma . . . Higbee."

I liked the sound of that.

He checked his notes again. "We'll begin with 'Abide with Me,' after which the invocation will be offered by Jedidiah Higbee."

Mr. Neeman didn't nod at Mrs. Billings, but she must have been accustomed to his haphazard conducting, because she launched into "Abide with Me" without any ado. The bass notes made my teeth rattle, but I liked her rowdy version (though it explained why Reverend Simms had never asked her to play).

We didn't have a song leader, but then, we didn't need one. There were just sixteen of us (well, seventeen with Mrs. Billings). After we finished the song, Daddy gave the opening prayer, but the only words I caught were, "Watch over his spirit as he ascends to Thee . . . again" and "Please bless our Ella Mae."

No sooner had he said "amen" than my hands began to sweat. Was I supposed to get up now, or would Mr. Neeman introduce me? I was about to leap out of my seat when Mr. Neeman stood back up.

"We'll now hear from Ella Mae, best friend of the deceased."

I wiped my hands off on my skirt, then made my way

up to the podium. The funeral-goers tracked my progress; I could feel their beady eyes crawling all over my back. I tried to picture them in their unmentionables like Miss Fightmaster had taught us, but they still seemed pretty scary.

The podium came up to my chin, so the younger Mr. Neeman dragged a stepstool out of nowhere. But when I climbed onto the stepstool, the podium came up to my waist. After considering my options, I positioned myself beside the podium. Once I was back on level ground—and within sight of Takuma—my heart stopped hammering.

"Good afternoon," I said. When I realized they couldn't hear me, I cleared my throat and tried again: "I mean, GOOD AFTERNOON!"

Chester laughed, actually laughed, but Auntie Mildred looked like she was about to blow a gasket. I could imagine what she'd say: *You're supposed to stand* behind *it, not off to the side.* Still, she didn't make a fuss, just gritted her teeth and bore it. Maybe Takuma's death had changed Auntie Mildred, too.

I dug my toe into the carpet. "I didn't write anything down, mostly because I couldn't think of anything, but I could talk about Takuma for the next ten years if I wanted to." When Theo's eyes bulged, I rolled my eyes. "But I don't want to, so don't worry."

Mama grinned, Theo relaxed, and a tiny smile even tugged at the corner of Uncle George's mouth. I drew a bracing breath. I could handle this, no doubt about it. After the last couple of weeks, I could handle anything.

"Mr. Neeman's right," I said. "Me and Takuma were best friends. But that doesn't mean I was the only one who loved him."

I sneaked a peek at Gracie (who blushed becomingly), then another peek at Mama (whose eyes were sparkling with unshed tears). They'd loved him differently, of course, but they'd loved him just the same. Comparing types of love was like comparing orange blossoms—every bloom was special just because it was unique.

"Some of us didn't love him," I went on. "Or at least we thought we didn't. But whether we loved him or not, he affected all of us."

This time, my gaze darted to Daddy (who looked like he was deep in thought), then to Auntie Mildred (who refused to meet my eyes). But I could tell that she was listening, since she was leaning forward in her seat and looking everywhere but at my face.

"Now, I'm not sayin' he was perfect—Jesus was the only person who was *that*—but it could be that Takuma was as close as you could get. I think that's why he changed us. He was like a mirror that way, reflecting our rights and wrongs back at us."

I hadn't meant to say that, but the words felt true enough, so I didn't take them back.

"Or maybe he affected us because of what he was. Maybe he knew things we didn't because he'd already died."

Auntie Mildred drew a nervous breath, and Miss Shepherd shifted anxiously, but I just plowed ahead.

"I don't know what he was," I admitted as I stared down at my toes, "but here's what I do know. He was kind and sweet and honest. He liked pork links and, according to my sources"—my eyes flickered to Theo—"Mildred Clausen's gingersnaps. He liked to sit and draw, and like Daniel, he was good at it. I brought a few to show you." I motioned toward the sketches—both Daniel's and Takuma's—that I'd hung on the back wall. "I call them *Memories of War.*"

The funeral-goers looked around. They probably hadn't even noticed the original artwork. Me and Mama had spent the weekend deciding which drawings to bring, and I thought we'd done a bang-up job.

"Well," I said, "I think that's it. Except to thank you all for comin'." I bowed, then added, "Are-ee-got-toe."

When I straightened back up, I caught Auntie Mildred's eye. I expected her to drop her gaze, but she jumped up instead. The crowd shifted away as if they thought she might explode, but she didn't go to pieces, just gripped the armrest for support.

"I'm not gonna lie," she said. "I thought that boy was trouble from the moment I laid eyes on him." She tilted to one side, but Gracie didn't let her fall. "I was so sure he'd killed Robby. It was the only explanation. So when I found out I was wrong, I couldn't help but wonder if maybe I'd been wrong about some other notions, too."

The truth was, Auntie Mildred was wrong about most things, but if she'd changed her mind about Takuma, maybe she could change her mind about the rest.

"It's gonna take time to adjust," she said, "but I *am* gonna try for the boy's sake. And for mine." She squeezed Gracie's hand. "God rest our immortal souls."

The silence that descended after Auntie Mildred sat back down was so perfect, so complete, that I almost didn't want to spoil it by taking two steps toward the casket. But I'd come for Takuma, not for everyone else.

His hair was neat and combed, and his skin was bright and shiny. He looked nothing like the pale gray ghost who'd coughed his life away, which made me think the Mr. Neemans were artists, too, in their own way. Still, something about him didn't look quite right to me. Maybe it was the makeup or the way they'd combed his hair. I could tell the Neemans hadn't known him when he was still alive.

"I'll miss you," I said, "but I know why you had to go."

After we sang a closing song, Mama gave the closing prayer. Once she said "amen," the service was officially over, but no one bothered to leave. They huddled in small groups instead, sneaking peeks at the casket when they thought no one was looking. Mama managed to ignore them as she cupped my cheek. She didn't have to say how proud she was; I could see it in her eyes.

Chester was finally brave enough to approach the wall of drawings. He walked up to one of Daniel's, the wide shot of the valley. Since Daniel hadn't titled it, I'd been referring to it as *The Sometimes Peaceful Place*.

I slipped out of my seat, but by the time I reached Chester, he'd already moved on to the second sketch, Takuma's crowded courtyard. He was bent cleanly at the waist, peering at it so intently that his eyes were slightly crossed.

"Careful, Chester," I whispered. "Wouldn't want your face to freeze like that."

Despite my attempt to whisper, he nearly jumped out of his skin. His forehead bumped the frame, knocking the whole drawing off balance.

"Sorry," he said, blushing.

"No, I'm sorry," I said. "I shouldn't have sneaked up on you."

He motioned toward the sketch. "It's just that the detail is so striking." He pointed at the nearest soldier (who was only an inch tall). "The men themselves are microscopic, but you can still make out their epaulets."

"What are epaulets?" I asked.

"The little doohickeys on their shoulders. Different ranks have different epaulets, so you can tell what their positions are just by their uniforms." He pointed at the nearest soldier. "If this guy were a Yank, he'd be a second lieutenant."

"I didn't realize you knew so much about ranks and uniforms."

Chester forced a nervous chuckle. "I guess that's just what happens when your dad dies in a war."

He probably meant it as a joke, but even so, I didn't laugh. "I'm sorry," I mumbled. "Have I ever told you that?" I lowered my gaze. "And I think Takuma would have been sorry, too."

Chester bumped me with his shoulder. "I should be telling you I'm sorry, not the other way around. He seemed like a swell guy."

"He was," I said, nodding.

Chester cleared his throat. "I guess Gracie thought so, too."

I hadn't wanted to mention it, but since he'd brought it up, I shrugged. "She liked him," I admitted, then sent him a sideways glance. "But I think she likes you, too."

"You really think so?" Chester asked.

I nodded solemnly. "And I think she's been waiting for you to make a move for a long time."

Chester's cheeks reddened. I thought he was going to pump me for more details, maybe get me to remember everything she'd ever said, but he managed to surprise me. "Well, I guess I'd better split. The boss only gave me thirty minutes. But I'm really glad I came." He nodded toward the podium. "The things you said up there would have changed anyone's mind."

My heart glowed like a live coal. A month ago, I would have called it pride, but now I hoped it was something more.

"Here," I said impulsively, easing the drawing off its hook. "I want you to have this."

"Oh, I couldn't accept that," Chester said. "It would break up your collection."

"I'll survive without this one. Besides, Daniel always said that art was meant to be appreciated."

He hesitated for a moment, then took the drawing with a bow. "Thank you," he said sincerely. "This might be the nicest gift anyone has ever given me."

"Then that's fittin'," I said, "seein' as how Takuma was the nicest gift anyone ever gave me."

Epilogue

One year came and went. It was May sixteenth again, the one-year anniversary of Takuma's birth and death. But the pain still felt razor-sharp. I tried not to think about him as I went through the motions of another Saturday, but the not-thinking was hard. Was this how Mama felt every time Daniel's birthday rolled around?

When I got home from helping Gracie fill out her college applications—she wanted to be a teacher, of all the crazy, mixed-up notions—I went straight to the kitchen. Maybe if we baked a birthday cake, I wouldn't feel so awful. But Mama was nowhere to be seen, and the kitchen looked so spotless that I couldn't help but wonder if Auntie Mildred had been by.

The one thing out of place was Daddy's copy of the *Times*, but that was strange all by itself, since he always threw away his newspapers once he was finished with them. It was almost like he wanted us to take a closer look.

I scanned the front-page headlines, but as far as I could tell, there wasn't anything unusual. I started to chuck it in the trash, but three letters—*DNA*—made me pull the whole thing back. I shuddered at the uninvited memory, then skipped back to read the rest: "WATSON AND CRICK DISCOVER CHEMICAL STRUCTURE OF DNA."

I had no idea who Watson and Crick were (though their names did sound familiar), but they must have been important. After drawing a deep breath, I hurried through the article as quickly as I could:

American James Watson and Briton Francis Crick have discovered the chemical structure of DNA, or deoxyribonucleic acid. "We've discovered the secret of life!" Crick is reported to have shouted after he and Watson solved the riddle that's been plaguing them for years. DNA determines eye and hair color, for instance, and according to Watson and Crick, it resembles a spiral staircase. They call it a double helix.

Watson and Crick made their discovery while working in Cavendish Laboratory at the University of Cambridge in Cambridge, England. The paper describing their research was published by the scientific journal *Nature* on April twenty-fifth of this year.
CONTINUED ON PAGE D4

As I flipped to page D4, I tried to figure out where I'd heard the word "Cavendish" before, but the memory wouldn't surface. At least it only took a second for me to spot the bright red circle at the bottom of the page. Daddy had clearly marked one of the paragraphs, but I started with the one before it:

> Linus Pauling, distinguished chemist at the California Institute of Technology, had nothing but admiration for the Cavendish pair. Though he published his own paper in February of this year, he called their discovery "a triumph." His paper suggested that the structure was a triple helix.
>
> But not everyone in Southern California's scientific community is taking the news so well. Victor Franks, a former researcher, had this to say about the matter: "James and Francis's research is purely theoretical and thus a thoroughgoing waste of time. The true visionaries in this field are putting these principles to the test in real-world applications, and we'll soon have a breakthrough of our own to announce."
>
> When asked to comment on Franks's statement, the Institute replied, "While it's true that Victor Franks was once employed by Dr. Pauling, he no longer works in any capacity at this university and does not speak on our behalf."

I set the *Times* back on the counter. Apparently, we weren't the only ones that Dr. Franks had lied to.

Before I could read the rest, Mama slammed the side door

shut. I wanted to ask her if she'd seen it, but I didn't have a chance before someone banged on the front door.

Mama cocked an eyebrow. "Were you expectin' anyone?"

Slowly, I shook my head.

"Me neither," Mama said, pulling her gloves off with her teeth. "But I guess we'd better answer it."

I bounced into the entryway and opened the front door. It had been a while since I'd chatted with a salesman. But it wasn't a salesman. It was a man with a striped hat (which was tilted smartly to one side). He had a pencil in his right hand and a notepad in the other, and his vest was stained and wrinkled, as if he'd slept in it for days.

"Mrs. Higbee?" he asked Mama.

"Yes, sir," she replied. It wasn't quite a question, but it sounded like one.

The man winked, actually winked, at me. "That must make you Ella Mae."

I stuck out my chest. It was about time that someone knew me just by looking at my face.

"I'm sorry," Mama said, bumping me out of the way, "but I don't think we caught your name."

He transferred the pencil to his left hand and offered her his right. "The name's Marty, Marty Crump. I'm with the *Los Angeles Times*."

She hesitated before shaking it. "Pleased to meet you, Mr. Crump."

Mama's unexpected courtesy put me instantly on edge, but he didn't seem to notice (or if he did, he didn't care).

"I'm very pleased to meet you, too. I've spent three weeks tracking you down."

Mama's eyes narrowed. "What do you mean, 'tracking us down'?"

Mr. Crump didn't reply, didn't even look up from his notepad. "As far as I understand it, you recently had contact with a Dr. Victor Franks of the California Institute of Technology."

Mama licked her lips. "Well, I wouldn't say *recently*."

"And he doesn't work there anymore," I said. "Or don't you read your own newspaper?"

Mr. Crump looked up from his notepad just long enough to smirk. "You're clever, very clever. Ever considered a career in journalism?"

I crinkled my nose. "Oh, no, I don't like journals. They seem too much like homework."

He batted that away. "I also understand that you took custody of a Mr. Takuma Sato, one of the subjects in his experiments. Would you say that's correct?"

"We didn't take custody," I said, thinking of Sergeant Friday, at the same time Mama whispered, "I think you'd better come in."

Her invitation caught me off guard—she didn't usually like socializing—but Mr. Crump seemed pleased as punch. He practically skipped into the house, his stained vest flopping merrily. I resisted the urge to shake my head. Maybe he could handle Mama's bark, but he'd never seen her bite.

"Sit down," Mama said, waving him onto the couch.

Dutifully, he sat.

"Now, let's get one thing straight." She stuck both hands on her hips. "I'm a reasonable woman, Mr. Crump, but if you're here to stir up trouble, I'll stuff that notepad down your throat."

His Adam's apple bobbed (though at least he had the good sense to return his notepad to his pocket). "I don't think you understand, Mrs. Higbee. I just want to talk."

"About Dr. Franks," she said.

"And Mr. Sato," he replied. "The records I had access to didn't paint the whole picture. For example, can you tell me exactly when and why he immigrated to the States?"

From the way Mr. Crump leaned forward, I could tell that this was why he'd come. He wasn't interested in Dr. Franks; he wanted to know about Takuma. If it had been up to me, I happily would have told him everything, but judging by the look on Mama's face, she didn't want to spill the beans.

"You've seen his passport, then?" she asked.

Mr. Crump's dark eyes lit up. "See, that's the thing," he said, scooting to the edge of his seat. "I can't find it anywhere. Not at the Institute, not at the morgue. I was wondering if you had it . . ."

He didn't have a chance to finish before Mama shook her head.

"Well, then, I'm in a bind." He mopped his forehead with his sleeve, partially dislodging his striped hat. "Now, I don't want you to think that I'm a lunatic or something, but it's as if your Mr. Sato materialized out of thin air when he turned

258

up in that lab." He sent us a sideways glance. "You wouldn't happen to know anything about that, would you?"

I gritted my teeth. It was like Mr. Crump already knew the answers to his questions and just wanted me and Mama to confirm them. But I wasn't interested in being Mr. Crump's source. Takuma wasn't a headline. He was a human being.

I sneaked a peek at Mama, and she sneaked a peek at me. Somehow, we both knew we were thinking the same thing.

Mama folded her arms across her waist. "I'm afraid we don't know what you mean."

"Give me a break!" Mr. Crump said, chucking his hat across the room. "This is the story of the century! You don't really want those Brits to take all the credit, do you?"

"Better them than Dr. Franks," I muttered.

Mama stooped down to retrieve his hat, then held it out to him. "I think you'd better go."

He jammed it on his head. "You're making a big mistake, you know that?"

"That's what they all say," I replied.

Mr. Crump started to answer, then wisely thought better of it. After sticking his pencil behind his ear, he stalked out of the house. His stained vest looked even worse from the back than from the front.

"Well," Mama said breezily as she slammed the door shut on his heels, "I don't think we'll be seeing the likes of him again."

"Good riddance," I replied as I collapsed onto the couch. My gaze flickered to the wallpaper, which was what it usually did whenever I made the mistake of spending too much time in the living room. The tiny pink rosebuds, forever on the verge of blooming, always made me think of *him*.

I plopped my chin into my hands. "It's his birthday, you know."

Mama sat down next to me. "I know."

My eyes started to water. "Did it ever stop hurtin'?" I peeped. "After Daniel passed away?"

She tucked one of my braids behind my ear. "No, it never did. But at some point in these last eight years, it did stop festerin'. Now it's a clean, smooth pain in the middle of my chest. I hardly ever feel it, only when I take a breath."

She smiled like she'd just said something funny, but I didn't feel like laughing. "Guess I have something to look forward to."

"I guess you do," she said, pushing herself back to her feet. When she reached the archway, she turned back. "But can I ask you a question?"

I didn't exactly nod, but I didn't shake my head, either.

"Would you ever want it to stop hurtin'?" More quietly, she added, "Would you ever want to forget?"

Not in a hundred lifetimes. Grudgingly, I shook my head.

"I didn't think so," Mama said. Once again, she turned to go, but she only made it a few steps before she turned around again. "What do you say we fry up a few pork links, just for old times' sake?"

"I'd like that," I admitted. "And I think he would, too."

Mama smiled her agreement, then disappeared around the corner, leaving me alone with the wallpaper and this sick feeling in my stomach. But it didn't feel as bad as it had a moment before. After all, pain was for remembering—and so were pork links.

Author's Note

This story started with one sentence: "Mama said it was plum foolishness to keep my cousin's dog tags like that, with his blood still stuck between the ridges of his name." It's changed a little since then, but the sentiment remains. I wondered what kind of character would say that line—and what kind of story she would tell—and *The Sound of Life and Everything* was born.

The Sound of Life and Everything is one-hundred-percent fictitious—as far as I know, it's impossible to do what Dr. Franks did—but the events surrounding his experiments were one hundred percent real. In the early 1950s, multiple scientists around the world, including Linus Pauling, James D. Watson and Francis Crick, and Maurice Wilkins and Rosalind Franklin, were racing to discover the chemical structure of DNA. Also, the anti-Japanese sentiment that existed in the wake of World War II was an unfortunate reality for many years. I simply combined these two pieces of history to tell Ella Mae's story.

While my fictitious Dr. Franks was bringing people back to life in the spring of 1952, Dr. Watson and Dr. Crick were doing their darnedest to determine the chemical structure of DNA. Since they knew the basic building blocks, they had scale models made—the "silly children's toys" that Dr. Franks speaks of—so they could try to construct it like a giant jigsaw puzzle. The overall structure eluded them until one day in late February of 1953, when Dr. Watson noticed that if you matched adenine with thymine and guanine with cytosine, the resulting pairs had the same shape. These pairs became the rungs that ran between the twisting rails of DNA's ladder-like structure, and with this riddle solved, they were able to complete their work in a matter of days.

You'll notice that I included Linus Pauling in the list above. He is the only historical figure to make an appearance in the book. Dr. Pauling studied chemistry at the California Institute of Technology from 1922 to 1925. Upon receiving his doctorate, he served there in multiple capacities, including as director of the Gates and Crellin Laboratories of Chemistry, from 1925 to 1958. Thus, while Ingolstadt Laboratories is a fictitious institution (which I named after the university that Victor Frankenstein attended in Mary Shelley's *Frankenstein*), I set the book in California precisely because of Dr. Pauling, as his were the only laboratories in North America that were competing with the research that was happening in Europe.

Like Ingolstadt Laboratories, the city of St. Jude is also fictitious. I didn't want to saddle an actual community with the moral highs and lows represented in the book. That said, Orange County is an actual location, and in the spring of 1952, it was mostly agricultural (though by the end of that decade, it had been taken over by suburbia, not to mention Disneyland).

Last but certainly not least, I should say something about Robby. I made a point of placing him in Company E of the 28th Marines, and specifically the small patrol assigned to take the summit of Mt. Suribachi, the highest point on Iwo Jima. I based Robby's experience on Richard Wheeler's eyewitness account, but Robby's actions were his own and in no way indicative of the way American Marines treated Japanese soldiers. Also, while I had to piece together a lot of Takuma's experience, I believe it is representative of the Japanese battle plan in general and Takuma's character in particular.

Acknowledgments

I don't know how you thank the people who've helped you achieve your lifelong dream, but since that's kind of the point, I'll do the best I can.

First, thank you to Kate Testerman, who not only plucked this story out of the slush but cared enough about this writer to establish a relationship long before that. I appreciate your tenacity as well as your optimism. I wouldn't have made it very far without either one.

Second, thank you to Shauna Rossano, who has championed this story from the start. Every writer should have an editor as exacting and encouraging as you. Also, thanks to everyone at Putnam, especially Jennifer Besser, and to Rose Wong for the beautiful cover.

My writing in general and this story in particular have benefited greatly from the expertise of fellow writers Amy Sonnichsen, Ben Spendlove, Jenilyn Collings, Kelly Kennedy Bryson, Liesl Shurtliff, Mónica Bustamante Wagner, Myrna Foster, and Tara Dairman. You push when I need pushing and soothe when I need soothing, and I can honestly say I wouldn't be here without you.

I also have to thank my parents, who never made me feel strange for wanting to stay in and write. I don't think books would be as important to me if they hadn't been important to you first. Also, thanks to Russell Walker, who helped with the Japanese. Anything I did right is your doing, and anything I did wrong is my fault.

Last but certainly not least, thank you to Chris, who lets me fret about my writing without fretting himself, and to Isaac, Madeleine, and William, who take me on grand adventures (and go on grand adventures by themselves when I need to get some writing done). You put up with the drama and get nothing in return, but none of it would matter if I didn't have you.